Angels in Disguise

Lou Dean

CLINESCOT
PUBLISHING
COLORADO

In the beginning of all things,
wisdom and knowledge were with the animals,
for Tirawa the One Above,
did not speak directly to man.

He sent certain animals to tell man
that he showed himself through the beasts,
and that from them, and from the stars
and the sun and the moon should man learn.

Pawnee Eagle Chief Letakots-Lesa

Thanks to Michael Phillips and Al Hartmann of the *Salt Lake Tribune* for front page coverage of the accident.

Thanks to "CBS This Morning" for inviting us on their show.

Back cover photo courtesy of *Vernal Express*
Edited by Giles H. Florence, Jr.
Cover design by Rebecca Porter

CLINESCOT
PUBLISHING
COLORADO

Blue Mountain Road, Dinosaur, Colorado

Printed in the United States

10 9 8 7 6 5 4 3 2

ISBN 1-56684-097-X

Foreword

I love my dog, have a healthy distrust of cats, and don't like stories about either of them.

So when I agreed to read Lou Dean's manuscript it was not the story that held intrigue for me—rather the author.

To me, Lou Dean was something of an enigma. A rancher, dressed in Wrangler denim and a studded shirt, she was gritty and strong—as are all those who raise and are raised off the land. Yet there was warmth and gentleness in her manner. What kind of writing, I wondered, would such an author produce?

The answer was rewarding. I found myself entranced, not in a strange-but-true canine story, but an outstanding work of literature. *Angels in Disguise* is a tender and masterful coming-of-age story about a little girl trying to find home, and about the invisible forces that tear us from home and tear homes apart.

There is genius in Lou Dean's writing. Her story is expertly crafted and poetically symbolic. Most importantly, her spirit emerges through her work with simple, honest, and poignant prose that endeared me as much to her as a writer, as to her story.

This is not a tabloid recounting of an actual event. It is a glimpse into a young girl's heart and perhaps into each of our own as well. And here lies the genius. For when I had finished her story I was left with more than a well-spent evening of literary enrichment and entertainment.

I was left with a yearning for home.

Richard Paul Evans
New York Times best-selling author

Acknowledgments

In my early years, an old Collie-Shepherd named Pat Dog patiently sat while I dressed her in my bonnets and bows. She listened intently as I taught her from the books I could not yet read. Thanks girl, for giving me my first taste of canine companionship.

Thanks to Shadow, the Coyote-Shepherd who appeared quietly one day on the old farm and because she endeared herself to Dad by killing snakes, remained with us for ten years. You helped me understand the value of knowledge by handing down your snake killing abilities to each litter of your pups.

Recognition to: Robie, the Great Pyrenees in Mountain Home, Idaho, 1970. You were abandoned by fate when your young master died in Vietnam. Our souls touched only briefly in our loneliness, but found love.

Special appreciation to Bambi, the toy Chihuahua who protected Scott and me during my single mother years. I can still see your face peeking through the curtains with enthusiasm when I walked in from work each day. Still feel you sneak against my neck at night when you'd leave Scott's bed and come to comfort my tears. I never understood how such a huge heart fit into that tiny body.

Mark Twain, you renewed my self-esteem after divorce, by your enthusiastic love and loyalty. Your Australian Shepherd energy and blundering ways brought laughter back into my heart.

Love to my present day family of Border Collies, Doubleday, Easy, Sissy, and Angel. With your intelligence and ability, you introduced me to the fascinating world of the working dog. Thanks for being on the rug nearby while I struggled with the writing of this book. For reminding me to break away so we could walk the hills together. Your patience while I muttered and complained. And for the confidence I could always see in your shining eyes.

Shorty, I still love you with my whole heart. During the difficult times your pawprints were alone on the creek bank.

On June 23, 1993, I died. It happened on our horse ranch above Vernal, Utah, at around five in the afternoon. A very special hero interrupted my journey toward eternity and allowed me to return to this world. Without his courageous effort, this book would never have been written.

1

THE DAY I TURNED FIVE, MAMA'S TERRIER CRAWLED beneath the chicken house and gave birth to a litter of pups. Dad was in high spirits that afternoon as he took the axe and began to cut a hole in the chicken house floor. The fact that a purebred like Missy had chosen such a "mongrel" spot to deliver amused him.

I knelt nearby and waited while my father reached into the darkness and pulled out the first pup. It was an exact replica of its mother, with Missy's black and white Manchester markings.

Mama took the pup and her face lit with triumph. "This is a fifty dollar pup. See, I told you I'd get the stud fee back and make money."

Dad, who'd been less than supportive of Mama's dog breeding venture, smiled as he lifted the second pup from beneath the floor. He dropped a brown and white speckled runt into my waiting hands and said, "Happy Birthday, Sissy."

"Don't say that to her, you know she wants a dog and I have to sell these pups to make a profit." Mama snatched the pup from my hands. "You know that too, Sissy."

For a brief moment my heart fluttered, stopped, then beat with a hammering slam as the argument continued.

"Well," Dad said, taking the pup from Mama and holding it by the skin over its shoulders. "Maybe you'd like me to dispose of it then. Looks like a drowner to me. Like a Beagle was somewhere in the woodpile," Dad said, "or a weeny dog."

Mama's eyes widened as she stared. The second pup was comical in appearance. He had the body of a Dachshund with the length and bowed legs, but his head was more Beagle and his spots were brown instead of black. He held little resemblance to his purebred parents. She reached under the floor clear to her shoulder and came back empty handed. "Just two?" She said, in astonishment.

Dad walked out of the chicken house laughing. "What a litter," he said.

Six weeks later, on a warm summer night we all sat outside snapping beans.

"Well, I think your mother oughta go into the dog business," Dad said, to no one in particular. "What do you all think? She could get us out of debt, pay off the farm."

Mama began to break green beans with a vengeance. "I

suppose every damn cow on this place is perfect, right? And every crop of wheat and hay? At least I sold the one pup, got my money back for the stud fee.

"What about the short-legged one with the long body?" Dad asked, humor high on his cheeks. "Want me to drown him for you? I'll be happy to drop him in the river tonight on the way to work." His words sent a shiver down my back.

Every night since the pup's birth, I'd sneaked out to see him after everyone in the house went to sleep. Every day that passed I clung to the hope that my chances for keeping him were improving.

"Maybe he's not even worth drowning," Dad continued, his voice still laced with amusement.

For the first time in my five years, I found courage. Something reckless rose up in me like a storm. I squared my slender shoulders. "He's my dog," I said. "His name is Shorty and I'm keepin him." Sis let out a little gasp of shock and Bub kicked me hard under the table. A long silence roared in my burning ears. The neighbor's coon hound called out long and loud down the river and a firefly winked across in front of us. "He told me so," I said, "that first day. In the chicken house."

Days went by and I expected at any given moment for Dad to scoop Shorty up and haul him off. Often when strays would wonder out to our farm Dad would load them into the back of his pick-up and drive them to Ponca City on his way to work. I always cried when it happened, because I'd gotten to know them and couldn't help wondering about their fate.

Another even worse fear plagued me at night. Dad talked often about drowning things. I'd never witnessed the brutality, but the image in my mind was enough. I could picture my sleepy puppy being snatched from his warm bed in the hay, dropped into a gunny sack and pitched down into the choking darkness of muddy water. I could feel the horror in his eyes and hear his squeaking plea for my help.

That summer, the arguing between my parents intensified. They seemed especially fond of it at night, when we were all in bed. I was a light sleeper and could never manage to smother the angry voices.

I began to sneak outside. I'd quietly unlatch the screen next to my bed and slide out. Shorty would always be asleep, just beneath my bedroom window. I'd pull a quilt out behind me, take my pup and go near the creek under the trees.

On one of those late summer nights, as I looked into the sparkling lake of stars overhead, I whispered a promise to Shorty.

"It'll be over my dead body," I said. "If Dad takes you, I'll be clingin to his leg. I won't let it happen, he'll have to drown me too."

In September I started school and Shorty followed me

every day. I'd tie him in the far corner of our field just across the road from our one room school house. At recess I'd take him sips of water in a paper cup and at lunch, teacher allowed me permission to cross the road and share my sack with him.

One afternoon Bub and Dad were loading a stack of pipe into the pick-up. Shorty and I perched nearby, watching as they worked and the sweat ran in little rivers down their foreheads.

Dad let out a howl and Bub yelled. Before I knew what was happening, Shorty dashed toward them. After a brief commotion, my dog squalled in a high pitched cry.

"I'll be damned," Dad said, scratching his head. "I'll just be damned, I've never seen anything like that."

When the dust settled, Shorty emerged from the ruckus with the biggest pack rat I'd ever seen. From head to tip of tail, that rat was as long as my little dog.

Everyone looked at Shorty with new respect in their eyes. I tried to contain my happiness, but my heart was flipping like a spring butterfly. The chances of my dog staying on the farm had just doubled. Dad was practical. He knew Shorty could be helpful to him around his shop and the barns, "he'd carry his own weight."

That night when I went to bed, Shorty jumped up and scratched the house just below my bedroom window. I waited until everyone was asleep, then, I quietly opened the screen and snuck out, dragging my quilt behind me.

When Shorty and I snuggled in together near the creek,

I thought about a time once when I'd been sick and Mama and Dad let me sleep on the couch with them both sitting on either side of me. I remembered them quietly visiting while the old wood stove wheezed and sizzled and a slow rain dripped outside from the roof. Being cuddled beneath the quilt with my dog was as warm as that one memory.

"You did a good thing, Dad loves a mouser." I told my buddy. "We don't have to worry now." But long after my friend's breath warmed my neck with the steady rhythm of sleep, I worried.

As the months passed, my fears about Dad began to ease. Shorty seemed to become an accepted member of the family—such as it was. The only photograph of us during that time was taken around 1953. It was brutally honest. Dad absent, Mama standing angry-eyed and thin lipped. Then the stair-steps. Lois Patricia, my eleven-year-old sis, with one shoulder shrugged down and a pre-adolescent smirk on her face. Bub, John Phillip, at nine, stood at attention, fists stiffly at his sides, military style. Me, at five, in a homemade dress and cowboy boots holding Shorty.

One day in late fall of that year, Mama left us kids with Dad. She announced that she was going to California to live with her sister and she did. Sometime after that Dad started making homebrew in the shed. The neighbor men stopped by often and Dad stood with them out by the barn and drank. He grew a stiff red beard, wore sweat-stained shirts and had an impatient edge to his voice. Shorty and I walked a wide circle around him.

Then as fast as Mama disappeared, she returned.

On a cold Saturday in February while us kids were ice skating on the pond in the far pasture, Mama gave all our pets away. Sis's dog, Ranger, and Bub's cat, and my Shorty, gone. I begged and bawled for days. I refused to eat and couldn't sleep, but no one seemed to notice.

One evening in March when the winds were still icy and the ground cold, Shorty came back to me. He had somehow gotten away from his new home and found his way to the farm. It was at night and I awoke to the sound beneath my bedroom window.

At first, I sat up, in a daze, convinced I'd been dreaming. Then the scratching sound came again and with it a familiar whine. I unlatched the screen and hit the ground with a thump. My friend ran around me barking in little circles, then jumped into my arms and put his head against my neck.

After that, Shorty stayed constantly by my side. Mama didn't seem to notice. He followed me to school every day and no longer had to be tied. Sometimes he'd chase rabbits or tromp the road ditches for field mice, but he was always in his place in the corner of our field at recess when I needed him.

A new teacher was hired that year. Miss Hedberg established her authority immediately by seating us alphabetically. We were bashful around her those first few weeks.

One morning, Mama woke us up, bawling. Over breakfast, she told us good-bye again and began to pack as we started off over the terraces to school.

Every few minutes during first period, I'd break my pencil lead so I could go near the window and use the sharpener. I'd crane my neck around and look to see if Shorty was still in the field, see if the brown station wagon was still in the drive.

When Mama's car disappeared past the school house in a cloud of red dust, I dropped my pencil and burst out of the old wooden doors. Feet flying, I ran toward the corner of the school yard, calling for my dog. When the spotted head popped up in the tall grass, I wailed out and Shorty sprang to his feet and ran to me. I picked him up and carried him to the school steps.

After a few minutes, the new teacher joined me. We sat for awhile in the warm breeze.

"You know," she said, "I've been thinking. That dog of yours comes to school every single day. Maybe he'd like to join us."

My heart quickened. "You mean . . . ?

"Yes," she said, "come, let's enroll him. If he's going to be here every day all day, he might as well learn something."

Shorty obediently lay by my desk for the rest of that school day. Miss Hedberg made the announcement during last period.

"Class, we have a new student. Shorty Jacobs, first grade, born right here in Osage County."

So Shorty became a permanent member of Braden School. Sometimes he'd go quietly to the big wooden doors and look back. I'd glance at Miss Hedberg for permission.

"Yes, you may be excused, Shorty," she would say, looking up from the blackboard.

When he'd return and give his little "Errff" she would stop writing on the board and allow one of us to let her "little canine boy" return to class.

At recess Shorty tolerated the young girls dressing him up and he played "chase em" with the boys. At lunch he'd get a sampling of peanut butter sandwich and oatmeal cookie.

In the afternoons, my dog and I lingered on the cement steps long after Miss Hedberg left and the noisy bus disappeared. With the company of the whistling wind, we'd cuddle beneath the giant brass bell on the porch of Braden School and escape into the security of our books.

2

MAMA LOVED THE WILDFLOWERS THAT COLORED THE creek in early spring. The blossoms stirred a lonesome yearning in me that year.

With Mama gone, Sis tried to make the transition to motherhood, nurturing us one minute and raving the next. Her introduction to puberty was harsh. She inherited the cooking, cleaning, and laundry before she turned thirteen.

In April I gathered the first bunch of delicate flowers along the creek and eagerly took them to Sis.

"What is it, Sissy?" she asked, impatiently, her face buried in a book of recipes.

"Mama always liked to put these little flowers in that vase, the one . . ."

"Mama isn't here," Sis said and, snatching the flowers from my hand, threw them in the trash. Then she plopped down at one of the table benches and began to bawl. "I hate this, I can't do it all." She covered her face with her hands and slapped her bare feet viciously against the linoleum floor.

Shorty and I picked another bouquet and offered them to Bub. "Mama liked these flowers an awful lot, Bub. Me and Shorty sorta miss givin them to her and we thought . . ."

"I reckon she's not missin em much now, Sissy," he said, stepping back from his work and wiping sweat from his forehead. "Start callin me Phil, would you, please?"

After that, Shorty and I ignored the early wildflowers. One day we took a weed sprayer from Dad's shop and killed a perfect bunch of Mama's favorite Iris out behind the granary. Then we cried and decided it hurt too much to think that Mama wasn't missing us. Not only did she miss us, terribly, but she was coming home. Shorty and I were sure of it.

That spring, the storms in northeastern Oklahoma were as chaotic as my emotions. Day after day, strong winds blasted through the trees, breaking limbs and leaving electric lines hanging. Almost every night, Dad shuffled us out the back door through a blinding rain and herded us into the safety of the cellar. For hours we'd sit by the kerosene lamp, playing cards while the winds raged above us.

After the storms, baby birds of every description floundered helplessly on the ground. I'd find them squirming along the creek banks in the mud, feathers drenched, bills opening wide, desperately begging for food that wouldn't come.

Shorty became adept at helping me locate the victims. He'd walk on one side of the creek bank, me on the other.

When he saw a bird, he'd sit, lift his head, and let out a mournful howl.

We developed a deep concern for the helpless creatures. I became a doctor and Shorty my assistant.

"Yes, doctor," I'd say to him, "this one certainly needs immediate attention. On a special little stretcher we made from a scrap piece of plywood, we'd scoop up our patient and run him off to the emergency corner of the chicken house, our hospital. We'd cover our ward with a clean white rag, dash out to dig a fresh worm, and return. We gave them all names and ages and some sort of description because they seemed so lonesome.

When the patients died, as they always did, Shorty and I buried them behind the chicken house. We fixed them up nice in one of Dad's cigar boxes, dug a tiny hole, held a service and then made a marker with name, date of arrival to the hospital, and date of death.

Shorty and I invited Sis and Phil to the funerals. They'd often come. It was a form of entertainment for them. I wore a cape of black tarp and a straw hat I'd blackened with Dad's shoe dye. I adorned Shorty with a collar made from black walnuts and bailing twine. I cried great buckets of tears when I shoveled fresh dirt over the grave and Shorty would howl. I gave last rites by waving a hawk feather in the air and singing an Indian song. "Ouga hooney, Shawm new." I picked it up from the Indians I'd heard in Ponca City. I had no idea what I was saying, but I loved the feelings that came with the sounds of the words.

Sis and Bub would sometimes chuckle, other times let

out great howls of laughter. Shorty and I ignored their stupidity.

My little "cemetery" steadily grew and became a family joke.

"If Sissy keeps running this hospital, I'm gonna have to buy more ground," Dad said one afternoon over supper.

"Yeah," Phil grinned. "You may need about a thousand acres if the storms are bad again this year."

Shorty and I tolerated their rudeness. We were on a mission and proceeded with pride and dignity. Our practice grew. We began to administer to the barn cats, chickens, calves, and lambs. When something needed special feedings, Dad gave the responsibility to us. Many nights Shorty and I awoke in the night to check the small piglet or lamb at the barn. Often in the wee hours when everyone else was sound asleep, we'd slip out of our covers, warm milk on the wood stove, and guide a bottle to an eager mouth.

The cemetery grew also, as bigger animals required larger plots. Before long the place behind the chicken house was overcrowded.

One morning in June, Shorty and I found a large baby bird struggling on the creek bank. The bird had his feathers and was much bigger and stronger than anything we'd ever found before, yet he couldn't fly. When I bent to put him on the stretcher, he fell on his back and extended two giant claws and let out a squall.

"This one might make it, Sissy," Bub said, kneeling and peering into the box. "He's too damned mean to die."

"What do you suppose he is?" I asked, intrigued by the new patient.

"Hard tellin but I'd guess some kind of hawk, with those claws and that beak, he's . . ." Bub got a strange look on his face. "I'll trade you out of him, Sissy. I'll give you my best shootin marble and . . . well my allowance for one week."

I looked at my older brother in pure disgust. I straightened my shoulders and turned to Shorty. "Have you ever heard of such a thang? Someone tryin to buy a patient? You can leave this hospital, please, and don't come back."

Bub made a face and left.

Days went by and it became apparent that after many months of failure, Shorty and I were going to be successful at saving a bird.

Our patient had a voracious appetite, snatching everything from worms to meat scraps from my hand. He would eat hungrily then retreat to the corner of his box. Bub came up with the name, Banchee and I liked the Indian sound of it. Banchee always greeted me and Shorty by falling over on his back, extending both claws in the air and squalling.

Phil became a regular pest. "I'll give you my army canteen and my three best catseye marbles and my shooter."

I'd always look into Shorty's unblinking black eyes for a reply.

"Shorty says, 'No.'"

One bright summer morning when we walked into the chickenhouse to feed Banshee, he wasn't in the box. A sinking fear started in my throat and trailed down my legs. So many times in the past I'd walked out to feed a patient and they'd be in the straw, lifeless. I swallowed hard and moved the straw around in the box. No bird.

Then from the corner of the building came a fluttering. Banshee dived through the air and landed on my arm. He jerked the meat scraps from my fingers.

Shorty barked and ran around my feet. I let out a hoop. Not only had our patient survived, he could fly.

But then, I noticed something strange. Our friend seemed to have some kind of new ailment, the feathers around his neck and on his head were thinning. My excitement turned into worry, was he sick?

After Shorty and I had become specialists in bird medicine, I'd spent three weeks' allowance money on a field guide of North American birds. All of us had taken a turn studying the pictures and descriptions since Banshee had survived. I began to look at the plates of large birds of prey, knowing that many young birds changed and took on different color as they matured.

I'd long since realized Banshee was a scavenger. Not at all particular, he'd grab anything from wilted lettuce to peanut butter sandwich and devour it without a thought. Reality hit me, as I stared at the plate on the American Vulture. My balding friend was a buzzard. I began to giggle when a new thought came into my mind.

Brother Phil had been especially mean that summer. It wasn't enough that he'd outgrown me all in one year and refused to play anymore. He took some kind of special delight in making my life miserable. Once at school he'd persuaded me to hide the principal's hand bell, then when Mrs. B was in a state of frenzy, paddle in hand, my brother told her I did it.

He had become a pain in little annoying ways, constantly saying, "betcha."

I could be talking about the simplest thing, like the weather, just making idle conversation on the way to school, such as "Looks like rain."

"Betcha," Bub would say, "How much you wanta bet? My best shooter against all your cateyes?"

Bub was always talking about "pay backs" to the neighbor boys. For some reason, getting even with someone seemed, in their minds to hold a certain distinction. They'd tell how they outsmarted a friend and then they'd laugh and pat each other on the back. The idea to get even with Phil took root and grew.

My brother hadn't given me a minutes' rest over Banshee. I'd never seen him want anything so bad. He liked to refer to Banshee as "Eagle" and his eyes would light with visions of power.

Although I'd formed a certain attachment to the bird, I knew he was a survivor and now that he could fly I figured Phil would turn him loose once he realized what he had.

"That bird is gettin to be a pain," I said one evening, loud enough for Bub to hear. He followed me to the chickenhouse and watched with renewed interest as Banchee stormed across, wings flapping, and landed on my arm. My pet gulped down wilted lettuce and pinto beans.

"You still want to keep him?" my brother asked. "Now that he's well?"

I played it very cool. "He does take up a lot of time," I said, cautiously.

Bub's eyes sparked. "Tell you what I'll do," He said, "I'll trade you my sleepin bag for him."

Shorty and I tried to hide our excitement. Bub's cushy sleeping bag had long been an object of our dearest affections. We slept outside all summer way up into the fall. Usually we'd wrap ourselves in a tight cocoon of quilts, but by morning our feet would be sticking out.

I didn't want to appear too eager. "What about your canteen?"

My brother's eyes narrowed. I knew I was pushing it.

"Done," he said, extending his hand. "Deal?"

We shook and I turned over full ownership of Banshee in exchange for Phil's army canteen and down sleeping bag.

During the next few weeks, Banshee's identity slowly became apparent to everyone. The few dark hairs on his head thinned into red skin and he grew into a slump-shouldered giant.

Dad laughed over the revelation and Sis started calling Bub the "Buzzard Keeper." Phil became so disillusioned with his treasure, he finally turned Banshee loose. But the buzzard had formed a solid attachment to my brother and returned, time after time, dragging scraps of snakes, rats, and other smelly trophies with him. Sometimes we'd hear him squawking out on the yard fence.

"Your buddy's calling you," Dad would say, then roar with laughter.

All of us had our share of fun with poor Phil who thoroughly deserved it. He never blatantly accused me of knowing, but he looked at me with a new respect and didn't tease me as much after that. When I began to call him Bub again, he didn't complain.

Mama returned unexpectedly in June that year. Dad seemed real glad to see her. Shorty and I acted surprised, but we'd known all along she'd return.

In October she made an announcement at the supper table.

"Sometime next April I'll be going into Ponca City and bringing home a little Jacobs' baby." She beamed and Dad reached over and gently patted her hand.

That night, cuddled in my sleeping bag I wiggled in anticipation of having a baby brother or sister. Grandma Carrie had visited us that spring. She talked a lot about God. Taught Shorty and me how to say our prayers at night and the importance of thanking Jesus ahead of time for things we needed.

Shorty decided this baby was a gift from God. He or she would surely be the thing to keep Mama happy on the farm. We said a long prayer of thanks for the blessing.

The next morning my dog and I resigned from the doctor profession. We cleaned out our corner of the chickenhouse and late that fall we used our allowance to buy flower bulbs and planted them over and around the little graves.

In the spring when our cemetery evolved into a blushing garden, alive with yellow daffodils, blue crocus, and multi-colored tulips, Mama went into the hospital.

Three days later, Shorty and I waited by the cattleguard when Dad brought Mama home. Both of us crawled into the cab of the pick-up. Mama placed the small bundle in my arms and pulled back the blanket. My fingers trembled when I reached and touched the mop of soft, red hair.

"Howdy, Lil Bub,"

Shorty sniffed the smell of new life and gently licked the top of my baby brother's head, then his tail beat against my leg and he stared up into my eyes. I winked at him. Our prayers had been answered. Mama was home for good and all the motherless creatures in our cemetery were in heaven

3

MY LITTLE RED-HEADED BROTHER WAS NAMED DAVID
Dean and I called him Lil Bub. While he was still in
training pants, Mama left again. This time she rented a
house nine miles away near Ponca City.

This departure was more devastating to me than previous ones. Not only did it shatter my faith in prayer, but at
about the same time Mama left, Shorty began to distance
himself from me. He would disappear and stay gone for
days.

When I didn't hear his scratch by my window, I knew he
was off on one of his trips and I worried. But he'd reappear
just as fast as he vanished, happy to be home, hungry and
tired.

"You're actin like Mama," I told him one evening, when
we crawled into the sleeping bag by the creek.

For the first time ever, he gave me an impatient glance
and had a far away look in his eyes that I didn't understand.

Dad said Shorty was a "traveling man." He said the words with a bragging kind of tone that further piqued my curiosity. When Bub grinned like a Cheshire cat and chuckled, my interest soared. I guessed it had something to do with the big S word. S for sex, silent sex. It chapped me that Sis seemed wise about things associated with those secrets and Bub did, but I was completely left out.

One morning our neighbor on the south appeared at the back door. Company was a rare event at our farm, so as Dad greeted the old man, the four of us kids crowded behind to listen.

"Come on in, Mr. Wilkens, have some iced tea."

"No sir, I've come to talk business," he yelled.

"What's the problem?" Dad asked.

Mr. Wilkens turned and pointed to Shorty behind him on the sidewalk. "This little dog belong to you?"

My heart stopped. If Shorty was chasing someone's stock or causing the neighbors problems, Dad would be furious.

"Belongs to the girl, yes sir."

"Well he . . ." Mr. Wilkens hesitated, looking past Dad at the four sets of curious eyes. "He jumped that bitch of mine. Purebred Beagle, she is. Papered. I paid big money for 'er and was gonna bred her to a pedigreed male."

A long silence ensued and I stood rigid with fear. "Was she penned up, Mr. Wilkens?"

"You damned betcha and that little bugger dug under the fence and was in the kennel with her yesterday morn, proud as a spring peacock."

Another silence. Thoughts of panic were causing me to fidget. Dad might shoot Shorty or haul him off or . . .

"Well then," Dad said, "you may be relieved to know that Shorty here is registered."

Mr. Wilkens turned and stared at Shorty who was watching the drama unfold.

"Yep, the wife paid $50 to breed her registered Manchester terrier to that pup's sire. We have the papers on him."

Mr. Wilkens, who had a reputation for pinching pennies, gave Shorty an appraising stare. "Well then, I reckon there's no real harm done."

"Truth is," Dad said. "Shorty is probably the only rat terrier in the county. As a mouser, I'd match him to any dog around. And he's a bit of a watch dog too, and smart. Ordinarily there's a stud fee attached to a dog like that. I'd say if that bitch of yours is worth a dime, those pups ought to bring fifty bucks apiece or more."

"Well," Mr. Wilkens said, backing off and quickly slapping his cap over his bald head. "Sorry to 've bothered you now. You be havin a good day, Mr. Jacobs."

When the old man disappeared down the sidewalk, Dad walked into the front room and wilted into his recliner. Little choking chuckles started in his throat and turned into howls of crackling laughter. All of us kids were grinning, but I was probably the happiest one in the room. For some reason I didn't quite understand, Dad not only wasn't mad at Shorty, he was greatly amused by the entire incident.

Over Labor Day weekend that year, we went to Ponca City to stay with Mama. The four of us trudged the quarter mile up the gravel road toward the cattle guard with our "over-night" paper sacks. Separation wasn't a cure for Mama and Dad's animosity. Dad forbid Mama to drive across his property line and she always pulled in, past the cattle guard, just far enough to prove she could.

When we returned on Tuesday morning, ready for the first day of school, Shorty wasn't around. I asked Dad immediately about my dog.

"Oh, he was here yesterday. I think. Or was it Sunday. Hell, I don't know, he'll be back."

At school, Miss. Hedberg asked about her canine student and I told her he'd be back soon, but my words didn't come out with any conviction.

That afternoon I walked miles to our neighbors' farms, searching for a glimpse of brown and white spots. No one had seen my dog. I slept by the creek that night, sobbing into my arm. I'd gone off and left him and he was in trouble.

The next morning I couldn't choke down the corncake in front of me.

"What's wrong with you?" Bub asked, cramming his mouth with bacon. All eyes focused on me.

"She's worried about Shorty," Sis said, nonchalantly as she dished up more hot syrup.

"That dog can take care of himself," Dad said, "you ought to know that by now."

The words helped in some small way, and I felt better

long enough to eat half of one corncake. But at school, I missed the warmth of my buddy near my feet. When kids began to ask about my dog, the fears washed over me again.

Finally even Dad began to wonder. He drove me around one afternoon to all the distant farms so I could ask about my dog. Shorty had built himself quite a reputation for "traveling" by then and almost everyone knew him by name. No one had seen him.

That night at the supper table Dad seemed almost happy about him being away so long.

"Ole Shorty must be making the rounds," he said, sipping his coffee. "Bet there'll be forty spotted puppies in Osage County this fall."

Sis and Bub fell into a grand chuckle while I frowned and glanced at Lil Bub, who was also excluded from the fun.

I decided it was time to become a part of the secret society. I hated being treated stupid and invisible. I knew by then they were talking about sex and that Shorty's visiting had to do with female dogs. I wasn't completely blind. I'd seen Dad borrowing a stallion to breed our mare and had carefully observed the bull in the pasture with the cows. I understood about such things.

It seemed like the perfect time to prove to everyone that I was old enough to join in their jokes. The week before, in front of the grocery store in Ponca City, I'd seen an interesting sentence written on the sidewalk. I knew it had something to do with Sex and the Silence, because when I'd pointed it out to Sis, she almost disjointed my arm by dragging me off. Then she completely ignored my questions as if she'd been struck deaf. I'd longed for an opportunity to use the words ever since.

With all the composure I could muster, I drew back my shoulders and broke the silence. "You're probably right. I'll bet my dog is out right now just _____ everything within fifty miles." The response was immediate. Dad sucked in a mouth full of hot coffee then spit it all the way across the kitchen. He let out a squall that rattled the dishes on the table then he jerked me up by the cuff of the neck, half carried, half dragged me to the kitchen sink and proceeded to wash my mouth out with soap and water.

Soon I was sitting back at the table in an atmosphere of strained silence. I'd seen Bub get his mouth washed out on several occasions and it looked horrid. I decided, sitting in the quiet, the punishment wasn't really that bad and somehow I did feel older inside, a true member of the secret society.

The next day I cornered Bub on the way to school. "What's that word mean?" I asked, getting straight to the point.

He stopped and grabbed me by the shoulder. "Don't you be sayin that, you hear." He walked a few fast steps then his expression changed. "Did any of the neighbor boys say that to you? 'Cause if they did, I'll whip every last one of em."

"No. I read it on the sidewalk in Ponca City."

"Well, don't be sayin words you don't know."

"Then tell me what it means."

He stopped again and frowned. "It's . . . you know . . . like *doing* it."

"Well, that's what I thought, see, so why'd Dad get so mad at me."

"Well, 'cause it's not nice. I mean. It's not like love and stuff. It's just the sex part," Bub said.

I was getting confused then. "What are you talkin about?"

"You know," Bub said, "Like Mama and Dad doing it, that was love but when . . ."

"What do you mean Mama and Dad doing it?"

He looked at me, shook his head and started off. "Forget it, Sissy. Forget I ever started any of it. Godfrey."

"Mama and Dad *breeding?*" I screamed the word out across the morning calm. Such a thing didn't seem at all possible to me. It was different with the animals. In my mind I couldn't comprehend people "doing it" especially not my parents.

Bub stopped. "Shut up," he yelled. "You are so stupid. How do you think we got here?"

"From the stork. Mama told me."

"Godfrey!" He turned and this time took off in a dead run.

That afternoon Bub came in to supper with a sheepish grin on his face. "I know where your dog is," he announced while Sis dished up beans and cornbread.

"Where?"

"He's been over to Billy V's house all this time. Charlotte Wilson started talkin about it today at school. Said this little spotted dog came limpin over to Billy V's one night at the river. Charlotte says Billy's been doctorin him and feedin him for nearly a month."

"Did you tell her to talk to him?" I was up on my knees on the table bench. "Did you tell Charlotte to tell him Shorty belongs to me?"

"Nope," Bub said. "'Sides Shorty will venture back pretty soon."

I stared at my brother then looked at Dad for help.

Dad finally wiped his mouth with the back of his hand and sipped his iced tea. "Reckon you and Sissy oughta go tell the boy," Dad said. "After all, it is Sissy's dog."

I nodded my head in agreement and smirked at Bub.

The next afternoon, Dad allowed Sis to drive me and Bub down river to Billy V's house. I was excited. Almost as excited to see the legendary Billy V as to get my dog back. In fact, I was irritated with Shorty. He'd gone too far this time. I'd been worried sick and he'd just taken up with some stranger and didn't miss me at all. His lack of loyalty was getting embarrassing.

The famous Billy V was the idol of every boy in Osage County. He didn't go to school but instead stayed home and took care of his grandfather who was blinded in World War II. For as long as I could recall I'd heard the boys talk about Billy V. Bub told about how he could piss all the way across Charley Creek and could smoke grapevines. Those sounded like dubious honors to me, but my brother was certainly impressed.

I had Billy V pictured as a big bully of a boy with a nasty look. When I climbed out of the truck and walked behind Bub to the small house, I felt smug. I'd come to claim what was rightfully mine.

Shorty met me first. He came walking up to me just as if he'd seen me the day before. Jumped up on my leg, yipped.

"You and I have a lot to talk about," I said, my voice firm with discipline. Shorty ducked his head.

"He's yours then?" The words were soft as buttermilk.

When I looked up, my breath stopped. I was staring into the most startling eyes I'd ever seen. They were the color of robin eggs, brilliant pale blue surrounded by lashes as dark and thick as crow feathers. When he smiled, both of his cheeks creased with fetching dimples.

"You must be Sissy?" He extended a brown, freckled hand. "I've taken real good care of him. He's a swell dog. When he first showed up he'd been in a fight and was awful chewed up. He's mended now."

My eyes couldn't move. My arms and legs hung heavy like I'd been poured and set in cement. "Well . . . I . . . I thank you," the words were stringy like taffy and I wanted more of them, so I didn't have to turn away.

"Well, see you, Billy V," Bub said, turning. He walked a few steps and realized I wasn't following. "Sissy, fetch your dog and come on. I got chores to do."

Billy leaned down, picked Shorty up and put him in my arms. Our hands touched and he looked at me again with those eyes. I was paralyzed.

"Good grief," Bub hollered from the truck. He took four giant steps back toward me, and started to give me a yank.

"You could keep him a while longer, if you wanted," I said. The words came out before they registered in my brain.

"I'd walk him over on Sunday," Billy said, "Would you like that, Sissy Gal?"

My heart was throbbing with the hum of the locusts in the trees. "I'd like it a lot, Billy V."

Bub listened, scratched his head and frowned. "Godfrey," he swore. "What's Dad gonna say?" Then he gave me a little push toward the truck.

Billy V raced along beside the pickup all the way to the highway with Shorty barking at his heels. Then he ran a ways farther, waving.

At dinner that night Bub explained that I felt sorry for Billy V and agreed to let him keep Shorty a few more days. Dad let out a grunt and started talking about the weather and the last cutting of hay.

That night when I wrapped myself in my sleeping bag out near the creek, I could feel those wonderful eyes, hear the voice, as gentle as soft rain. The freckled hand reached out and lifted me into my dreams.

Billy V came with Shorty late Sunday evening after supper. He sat for awhile with me and Bub and had lemonade. Bub chattered about Army things and Billy kept glancing at me, talking to me with his eyes.

When he started to leave he picked Shorty up and put

him in my arms. "You watch after Sissy Gal, you hear?" He rubbed Shorty's ears and walked off a few steps, then turned. "Reckon I could come see him now and again?"

A nod was all I could manage.

He left, reluctantly. And I knew, as he walked then stopped and glanced back, that he didn't want to leave me and that knowledge sent my heart clattering.

"Billy V ain't actin' like his ownself," Bub said, scratching his thick hair. Then he walked off toward the barn.

Shorty settled in my lap as if he'd never been away. I had a dozen things lined up to say to my dog, but as I watched the distant figure fade into a speck against the setting sun, I remained silent. Now I understood why Shorty roamed, that far away look he had in his eyes sometimes.

My belly twisted into a tiny snake and crawled behind a rock inside of me. In that moment I also knew what Bub had said was true. Mama and Dad had done sex just like the other animals and as a result, us kids had been born like the calves and the colts and the lambs.

Shorty and I sat together until the dim light faded into darkness. The June bugs began to hit against the porch light, the tree frogs sang, and the fireflies winked.

And although I'd sat a hundred summer nights like that and seen and heard the exact same things, on that summer night, in 1957, I buried my face in my dog's neck and cried, because everything was new.

4

BILLY V VISITED ME EVERY SUNDAY AFTERNOON FOR SIX weeks.

It soon became obvious to my disbelieving brother that Billy was coming over not to talk Army with him, but to see me. Before long everyone at school whispered about it. I lived for Sunday afternoons when the two of us would sit at the splintered picnic table and sip lemonade.

Shorty would walk with me and Lil Bub to meet Billy near the Charley Creek Bridge. My dog was as smitten as I was. He greeted Billy warmly with his little "Errf" then jumped on his leg. While we sat in the yard until late evening, Shorty lay contentedly with his head in Billy's lap. Sometimes Billy and I would play cards with Lil Bub. Stealing glances across the table, we'd brush our fingers together at every opportunity.

Dad was greatly amused with the romance and called me Juliet, which caused my ears to burn. Sis said Billy was trash and would never amount to anything because he didn't attend school. But nothing could dim the strong feelings that started the first day I looked into his striking eyes.

And, nothing could prepare me for what would happen next. One Sunday Shorty and I walked to Charley Creek and waited, but Billy didn't show up. Bub told me, nonchalantly, the next day, that Billy V had moved to Arkansas. I had no idea how much space he filled inside me until he left. The emptiness consumed me for weeks. My appetite left and sleep came only in fretting stitches as I reached for the freckled hand.

Slowly, I let go of my beloved Billy, little by little, Sunday by Sunday. But anytime Shorty and I visited Charley Creek Bridge, the snake inside of me stirred from behind the rock. I told Shorty I'd never fall in love again. Although the joy was the sweetest thing I'd ever tasted, I didn't want seconds on the pain.

One Saturday in early fall, we all rode into town to buy groceries. Our monthly trip provided basic necessities and feed and salt for the animals. We had a set ritual. All of us cleaned up, Dad spread a quilt in the bed of the pickup. Sis rode up front and the rest of us rode in back. After Sis and Dad came out and set the boxes of canned goods, beans, sugar, and flour around us, we followed them into the Woolworth Store to spend part of our monthly allowance.

On that particular afternoon, while Sis and Dad bought groceries, I sat on the spare tire, head in hands and stared around at the few people passing in and out of the grocery store. Bub was reading a brochure on the Air Force while Lil Bub played with a pair of roly-poly bugs he'd brought from the farm.

Shorty sat beside me, snapping at a persistent fly, while we read silently from my Oklahoma history book.

And Geronimo rose to chief of the Chir . . . (um) *ica . . .* (um) *huas following the death of Cochise. Pitted against almost impossible odds, he continued to fight the white soldiers long after most Western tribes had been forced onto reservations.*

Still staring at the words, I began to fantasize about this man called Geronimo. I liked his spirit. I sat for a few minutes and visualized being Geronimo, forced to leave my home in Arizona and move to Oklahoma.

"When the Bookmobile comes to school next week, we'll check out everythang that's been written on Geronimo." I whispered to Shorty.

Out of the corner of my eye, I caught sight of an old Ponca Indian making his way slowly from the alley. He had a bright blanket of red and yellow slung over his stooped shoulders and his raven hair, now streaked with gray, was braided into a long twist down his back.

While Bub read and Lil Bub played, I focused on the Indian man and watched with unblinking eyes. He stood ever so still and erect for quite a spell then all of a sudden, he began to sing. His voice growled out a song that made a knot hang in my throat. The words came from somewhere deep inside him and sounded like pain and anger and fear.

"Bub," I said, wanting to share the feelings that were stirring me, "Look. Listen."

"He's drunk," Bub said, glancing up then looking back into his pamphlet.

When the old man began to dance, scuffing one moccasined foot in front of the other, he stumbled, then fell over onto the curb and puked. Without hesitating, I jumped over the side of the truck and hit the pavement running.

"Sissy, get back here," Bub said, grabbing for me.

The old Indian sat up and looked at me with smokey eyes from beneath leathered lids. Something in his face softened.

"You okay?" I asked.

His wrinkled lips twitched ever so slightly. His eyes didn't move from mine. My fifty-cent allowance was squeezed firmly inside a sweaty fist. I had plans for popcorn and a strawberry soda pop. But a great flood of empathy welled up inside of me and I felt compelled to give something to the old Indian. Before I could change my mind, I pushed my fist toward him and opened my fingers. The two quarters landed then disappeared into the dark palm.

The smokey eyes blinked, then stared in silence. He reached slowly into his vest pocket and drew something up. He dropped the copper coin into my hand. I stared in disbelief at the Indian-head penny. He pushed my hand toward me and grunted. We'd made a trade.

Just as I was thoroughly enjoying the excitement of the moment, Bub's large hand came down firmly on my shoulder and he pulled me to my feet.

"Get away, Bub, this ain't your business." I said, feeling pretty important.

When he began to drag me away, I let out a squall and when he started to pick me up I kicked him hard on the shin. He cursed and twisted my arm behind my back. When I screamed, Shorty dived out of the truck and started for Bub.

Dad appeared out of nowhere, red-faced and frowning. He caught Bub and me by the arms and started hauling us toward the truck. Shorty attacked Dad. Grabbing the hem of his overalls, my little dog shook and growled like he was flopping a rat. Dad let out a howl and dropped me and Bub half-way into the pickup bed. He reached and got Shorty by the scruff of the neck.

"Little dog," he said, tossing Shorty into the truck. Then he turned his attention to me and Bub. "What in the hell are you two doing out of the truck?"

"Sissy was messin around that old . . ."

Dad held up his hand. "Never mind," he said, "Just never mind."

He looked down at Shorty, who was still bristled up. My dog raised his lip to Dad and growled. But instead of Dad getting more upset, he gave a short laugh.

"Little dog, I like you, I really do. But there's something you best remember. You mess with the old man again and there won't be anything left of you but a greasy spot."

Shorty stared for another minute then crawled into my lap, content that the fighting was finished. When we backed away from the curb, my old Indian friend stood by the light post, staring straight ahead. I waved frantically, but his cloudy eyes didn't blink. I settled in a corner and examined my Indian-head penny. When Dad stopped at Woolworth's and Bub jumped with Lil Bub to go in, I went along. I decided not to show anyone my treasure in fear Dad might take it away from me, so I went on in with the boys and acted like I was saving my allowance for Christmas.

When the boys bought crackerjacks and strawberry pop, it didn't bother me. I held my penny tight in my fist and followed along behind them, grinning.

As the fence posts blurred by on the way home, Shorty and I thought about Geronimo and the Indians. We'd been studying about how they were uprooted all across the country and moved into Oklahoma. I sneaked a quick peek at my penny. The date below the Indian's head was 1899. My imagination flamed with curiosity. I was born in 1948. In the soft dust on the rim of the spare tire I subtracted. The penny was forty-nine years older than me.

Then, my thoughts jumped back to the old Indian. I knew that his song had something to do with a yearning for things past. That date, 1899. Was Geronimo still holding out against the White Soldiers then? I had to know.

By the time school let out in the spring of that year, Mama and Dad had been officially divorced for six months, and Mama was remarried to a man named Hank. Lil Bub and I went to visit Mama and Hank in Shawnee,

Oklahoma. Mama had been writing to us for months about how they had a nice place in the country with a swimming hole and a place to fish. Sis was going to spend the summer in Arkansas with Aunt Eunice and Bub was helping Dad on the farm.

Reluctantly, I told Shorty good-bye and gave him a lecture about traveling too far away from the farm. We were only going away for two weeks, but Shorty had a way of getting impatient in a hurry.

The day Mama picked us up, I got an uneasy feeling about the visit. She kept acting weird on the way to Shawnee, then when we arrived, I noticed all of their stuff packed in big boxes.

"Why haven't you unpacked?" I asked.

"Oh, some of that stuff is just things we don't use," Mama said.

I wasn't satisfied. Life with Mama was never that simple. A few days into the visit, Mama sat me and Lil Bub down at the kitchen table. "Hank's been transferred to Muskogee," Mama said, "so guess you guys will get to help us move."

"Well," I said, concerned about getting too far from home. "How far is Muskogee?"

"Not far."

So off we went to a town half-way across the state.

Before the two weeks passed, I was getting homesick. The past few months I'd gotten more and more attached to our Palomino mare, Maybelle. She'd been given to us by Dad's sister, our Aunt Eunice. Although Sis claimed her, I often talked to Maybelle as I brushed her. My riding time, for several years had been limited to stolen moments in between Sis's plans. But recently, when my sister's interest shifted from horses to boys, I began to snatch more time with the horse.

My new love of Indians added to the passion for a horse of my own. I fancied myself a rebel Apache. The white soldiers were my enemies. For weeks before we'd left with Mama, I'd painted myself with berries and ridden Maybelle, bareback. Dad began to call me Geronimo and named Shorty, Running Short. Riding the big golden mare, crashing through the brush, climbing hills and hiding in the gullies connected me to the past, to the pain of my old Ponca Indian friend, and to freedom.

Maybelle was pregnant and going to foal in late June. I'd taken on the responsibility of closely watching her, checking every day to see she was brushed and pampered. Even though the foal belonged to Sis, I felt a special anticipation for the coming event.

With Sis gone to Arkansas for the summer, I worried about a lot of other things too. If a piglet was rolled on by the sow or a twin lamb was destined to be a bum, it was usually Shorty and I that noticed. Dad and Bub stayed so busy, they often didn't have time for such things.

After another week passed, I asked to go home.

"I talked to your Dad, he and Phil are busy harvesting and Pat's living in Arkansas. He thinks it's best for you and Davey to spend the summer with us."

The news devastated me. I ached to know if Shorty was all right. I missed Maybelle and all the animals on the farm. And somehow, deep in my gut, I knew Mama wasn't being completely honest.

After six weeks, I accepted the fact with brooding silence. I convinced myself, somehow, I would make it through the summer. Lil Bub seemed contented enough, although he also asked often about Dad and the farm. The two of us spent our days playing hop scotch and marbles on the sidewalk in front of the small house. The only joy of the summer was the small library three blocks away. Every week I came home with my limit of books.

In 1894, Geronimo and his remaining Chiricahuas were taken to Fort Sill, Indian Territory. By 1899, the great warrior was defeated, turned into a human exhibit. As I read the words, I clenched the penny to my heart.

Homesickness for my dog choked me every day. My connection to the Indians was deeper now. I understood the pain of feeling misplaced, the anger that couldn't escape. Often I'd awake in the night, climb the tree and sing the Indian's song, the way I remembered it.

One particular night, I awoke in a sweat, tangled in damp sheets, dreaming I'd heard Shorty whining beneath my window. Then I realized I wasn't on the farm and knew my little dog was scratching on my window at home, wondering where I was.

I walked softly outside to the splintered porch and stared at the summer moon. I let my voice rise and fall with the pain, anger and fear, scuffing one bare foot and then the other in a small circle, whispering the words in the darkness. The song was a promise that if I ever got back to my Shorty, to Maybelle, the cows and cats and lambs, nothing could ever make me leave again. The farm was my haven and my heart. Like Geronimo, I'd never stop fighting for my home. I sang and danced and drove the White Soldiers of fear from my mind.

"A wooney balla caw. Soma sina woo choo."

When Mama would talk to me, I'd get quiet inside and stare at her with a squint, letting my pain take me to my promise. The power of my secret was something she'd have to deal with in her own time.

In late August Lil Bub and I were eating a bowl of cereal one morning when I saw my dad walking up the steps. I jumped and ran to him, squealing with delight. He lifted me up and reached and ruffled Lil Bub's hair. Mama came out behind us.

"You can't take them," she said, "I'm putting them in school here."

Dad's face was scarlet and his blue eyes narrow. "We'll leave that up to the kids," he said. Then looking down at me he said, "Sissy, you want to go back to the farm or stay here."

"Home," I said, without hesitating.

"Me too," Lil Bub said.

"Run and get your stuff," Dad said, giving me a little push.

While I was stuffing clothes into our ragged suitcase, I heard my Dad's angry voice from the porch. "If you ever pull a damn trick like this again . . . I swear I'll never let you take them off the farm or even see them."

Mama cried as we drove off. In the deepest part of me I cried for her. I felt sorry that we had to leave like that, but angry, because I knew then, for sure, my intuition had been right. She hadn't talked to Dad at all. He'd spent the entire summer looking for us.

Shorty met me with excited barks and ran in tight circles around me until I fell down in the grass. I touched his face, ran my fingers gently down his back, tracing his bow legs to his feet. He snuggled on my neck and whined out his sleepless nights and long days of worry.

Phil and Pat changed a lot that summer. Sis gained about fifteen pounds in woman places and glowed with a look of health. Boys began to come visit her in twos.

Bub had become a man in three short months. His feet were bigger than Dad's, he was nearly as tall, and he had the hint of a mustache. He didn't play Army or baseball anymore, but always had his head under the hood of Dad's old truck with the engine running and the radio blaring.

Dad had lady friends calling and coming to the farm. He had closed down the homebrew still, shaved his stubble beard and the harsh edge to his voice had softened.

I tried to escape to see Maybelle that first afternoon, but Dad made me unpack and help Sis in the kitchen. I asked Dad and Sis about the foal. Had Maybelle had her colt? Was it okay? They ignored my questions which left me with an uneasy feeling.

Then, over supper, Dad said, "Since we missed your birthday, I guess we better do something about it now." He handed me a card and I thanked him, laying it beside my plate.

"Go ahead, open it," Sis said, her eyes eager.

When I gently broke the seal on the envelope and pulled on the card, I expected a few dollars to come sliding out. Money never excited me much. I preferred a surprise present of any kind. Instead of money inside, I found an index card printed with Dad's bold hand printing.

Maybelle had her foal in June, a few days after your tenth birthday. It's a filly and it's yours. Happy Birthday!

I read the words slowly, then faster, my breath stopped. I looked into Dad's eyes. He was grinning.

"You mean . . . she's mine? A filly. My very own horse?"

Dad nodded, taking a long sip from his iced tea. "Sis and I planned it from the beginning. Since Maybelle has always more or less belonged to Pat, we figured, the foal should be yours. If . . . well if you'd been here this summer, we would have told you on your birthday."

"May I . . . be excused?" I asked. When Dad nodded again, I quietly scooted out of my place on the bench, softly tread across the floor, then blasted out the screen door with a bang. I barely touched the ground between the house and the barn, my eyes scanning the distance, searching for a glimpse of the big palomino mare. Shorty was yelping at my heels.

Down to the creek behind the barn, around to the pond, up across the terraces, bare feet oblivious of sandburs and wheat stubble. Then, in a thicket of blackjack trees, we spotted them.

Maybelle's head came up and she nickered a welcome. I took small deliberate steps. Soft steps, my breath pounding in my ears. The tiny filly pranced around Maybelle and stopped, spraddle legged, staring. I held out my hand and she whiffed it with a nervous breath. I knelt down in the grass so she'd relax and get used to me. Shorty crawled in my lap and slept.

We stayed until dark. Looking. Filling our eyes with the delight. The foal was deep red sorrel with flaxen mane and tail. She had white stockings and a bald face. Before I left, I ask Shorty what he thought of the name, Princess. We agreed it fit her, because she was perfect in every way.

Shorty and I waded down the creek on the way home. For the first time in weeks, my mind went to Billy V. The thought of him no longer churned the feelings inside me.

5

By October I was riding Maybelle again, walking her slowly through the pastures and along the creek bank with Princess, and Shorty following. When the leaves began to turn that year, our world flashed with the bright reds and golds of change.

Mama and Dad were never going to be together again on the farm. Shorty and I knew it was time for us to give up that prayer. Mama had a different husband and a new life. Dad had lady friends, Sis was dreaming of marriage, and Bub kept talking about the Air Force.

One brilliant autumn Saturday, I took off my shoes and shirt and painted my face and upper body with pokeberry juice. Then I used the stain to mark Maybelle and Princess and Shorty. We walked up to the highest point on the farm, the hill beyond the pond. I whittled myself a homemade spear and ate wild garlic and held my penny tight. I thought about the old Ponca Indian—about the journey that brought him to that curb that day, drunk, about his beginnings.

As the wind clattered through the stiff leaves and the sun reflected off of golds and browns and reds, I wailed out my fear and my anger and my grief. Everyone else could do what they had to do, but I'd remain forever on the farm with my animals.

I screamed out the promise, from the deepest part of me, my high pitched voice piercing the autumn wind. Shorty's shrill howl whined out in chorus.

And inside, Shorty and I became Geronimo. Alone. Running. We were an island. The rest of our tribe had forsaken us and gone to the reservation, but we would never leave the land.

I jumped on Maybelle and motioned for Princess and Shorty to follow. The four of us crashed through the blackjack trees and stood breathless, hiding. We let the White Soldiers of fear pass by then rode to freedom.

By the spring of 1959 at eleven, I was barefoot and usually shirtless. My dog and I ate, slept, and played together.

Mama and Hank had bought a home in Texas. When she wanted to see us that Easter, I visited her briefly at the cattleguard, then climbed on Maybelle and waved to Lil Bub, Sis, and Bub who were going with her to Ponca City for the night.

I ran Maybelle as fast as she'd run toward the blackjack thicket on the far side of the farm. I painted my body with pokeberry juice and held my Indian penny. Then I built a small fire near the creek and sat cross-legged with Shorty in my lap. I prayed to the spirits and to Mother Earth, who

I'd accepted as my new guardian. I grieved over Mama, over the trust that she had killed and I buried the loss.

Shorty and I fought the White Soldiers and won.

That spring the rain came with gentle passion. The creek behind the house overflowed its banks flashing up into the back yard with violent swiftness. Us kids put on cut-off jeans and dived into the cold waters with shrill screams of joy. We sat on the banks in the late afternoon and watched the huge soft shell turtles come floating down, visiting us from the Arkansas River. We caught catfish and fried them crisp with hush puppies and picked fresh poke and boiled it gently into soft greens.

When the rains stopped, Dad put us to work painting gates, cleaning fence rows, and picking up limbs along the creek. By late spring the farm glistened with wildflowers, redbuds, peach trees, and lilacs. We spent many hours in the garden and yard and orchard. While I worked, Shorty waited somewhere nearby in the shade and Maybelle and Princess munched tender grass beneath the trees. Life was safe again.

The first tremor of change came one late afternoon when I started in to help Sis with supper. I heard Dad's voice before I stepped foot into the yard.

"This guy has already been married and divorced and has a child, Pat. You better listen to what I'm telling you. You're buying yourself problems."

"I'm in love with him and we're gonna get married whether you accept him or not."

I stood barefoot on the path and my heart stopped. Sis had been dating lots of different boys for the past year. They came and went and I paid little attention to any of them. If she was getting married to someone, I knew it meant changes. I'd now be alone in the house to do the cooking and cleaning all summer. And although the thought of having that responsibility didn't scare me, I knew it would cut deeply into my free time in the hills with my animals.

"Well, I guess you're right. You'll be eighteen soon. I can't stop you. I just wish you'd give it more time. I don't have anything against Gene. He seems like a nice enough young man, but . . ."

"I'm glad you feel that way," Sis's voice faded and I walked quickly toward the house so I could hear what else she was saying.

"You did what? When? For hell's sake, Pat."

"We're married," Sis said. "He's rented an apartment in Ponca City. I'm moving out today."

When the silence went unbroken for ever so long, I finally squeaked the old screen door open and went inside. Dad was sitting at the table, clinging to a mason jar of iced tea.

"Your sister ran off and got herself married. She's moving out." Dad said.

"Well, I can do things, you know. Cook and clean and we'll get along fine. You and me and the boys."

Dad nodded, without much enthusiasm.

"I'm just going to be in Ponca. Gene and I will come out every few days and I'll help." Sis offered.

Again Dad nodded, with the same lack of energy. Then he stood, grabbed his cap from the peg on the back porch wall and let the screen door slam with a thud.

Somehow, we managed after Sis left. Dad would decide the evening before what we'd eat the next day for supper. Bub began to take an interest in the kitchen and before long, he was doing most of the cooking, which allowed me some free time between school and dishes. Then Lil Bub would pitch in and help Bub with his barn chores while I cleaned up the kitchen and straightened the house.

Sis and Gene came out often on Sundays. My older sister taught me the secrets of crisp fried chicken and pan gravy. She helped me with the laundry, starching, and ironing. Sis laughed a lot and looked at Gene with lingering eyes.

And for the next few months, we did do just fine. Bub and I had a few good-natured scuffles, but we had a lot of grand times in the kitchen singing and cooking. Lil Bub was getting big enough to be a fair help in the house and the garden. By July, he'd taken up with one of Bub's piglets and spent hours at the barn yard with his "Mr. Grunt."

Dad was taking a lot of mysterious trips to Purcell by then.

He'd sometimes leave us at Sis and Gene's apartment for the weekend or they'd come to the farm. Once he took me and Lil Bub with him and we all stayed at Grandma Carrie's. Dad left on Saturday and returned with a lady friend named, Anna. He introduced us, and I noticed he looked at her the whole time with a soft expression in his eyes. A streak of fear started somewhere down deep inside of me and boiled around in my middle until I felt sick.

A month later, Bub and Dad got into it late one afternoon.

I'd been riding Maybelle and was just coming in when I heard them.

"I've told you, Lad, as long as you're under this roof, you won't smoke those cigarettes. Now let me have them."

I stood frozen, my hand on the screen door. A scuffle of noises came from inside.

"Oh, so it's come to this, huh? You think you're bigger than the old man? Well, okay, Lad, just lay one on me."

I heard a quick thump and a crash, then Bub came shooting out the back door and disappeared, running up across the field. When I walked inside, Dad was pulling himself off the floor and wiping blood from his face. He walked to the sink and started splashing water on his face then held a damp rag to his nose and lip.

"I'll be go to hell," he said, moving his nose around with his fingers. "I didn't really think he'd do it."

Bub didn't come back for a week. When he did, Mama was with him and he told Dad, in front of me and Lil Bub, that he was joining the Air Force when he turned seventeen in September.

"You can't do that unless I sign for you," Dad said.

"Mama already has," Bub said. "And I'm gonna live with her until I leave for boot camp."

That second tremor of change caused aftershocks in my heart for several weeks. Sis was married. Bub was going off miles and miles away to be in the Air Force. I spent every possible free minute on Maybelle, streaked with pokeberry juice, roaming the hills with Shorty always in sight.

In late August, came the quake that crumbled my world into chunks of debris. Dad sat me and Lil Bub down one morning and made an announcement. "I'm marrying Anna and we're moving to her house in Purcell."

After the terrible news settled upon my mind like heavy mud slung sloppily against a barn wall, I managed to speak. "But . . . she lives in town, doesn't she? What about Maybelle, Princess, and the dogs? Mr. Grunt, the lambs, Kitty Tom . . . ?"

Dad waved off my concerns with a flip of his wrist. "It'll work out. We'll find a place to pasture Princess. You can take Shorty."

The day of the auction, I sat beneath the willow tree and held Shorty tight. I stared, blindly at strangers milling and picking through piles of things that the day before had been ours. Tossing, grabbing, yelling out bids. Each time a vehicle left, I wondered which of our possessions they had hidden inside. When I watched Maybelle disappear in a cloud of red dust, her eyes wide and wild from the back of a horse trailer, I stumbled away. I went to the far side of the place where I couldn't hear the voice of the auctioneer or see the traffic leaving. I painted myself and Princess with pokeberry juice and stripped off my shirt. I held my Indian penny tight and scuffed my feet in a tight circle and began to moan.

From places inside of my soul yet undiscovered, came sounds that I had not yet heard. I said good-bye to Maybelle, my friends the birds and the lambs and pigs and calves. I grieved for the creek, the oak trees, and the hills. Falling to the ground, I wrapped my fingers in the grass, clinging to Mother Earth. I remembered my old Indian friend on the curb and now completely understood the depth of his pain for the first time.

When I returned to the house, Anna told me I had to wash and handed me a blouse. "You're a young lady now, and much too old to be going without a shirt."

I walked to the creek and washed, put on the blouse and sat cross-legged in the yard, watching the few remaining people leave with our treasures. Shorty whined in my lap.

The white soldiers had won. The only thing left for us was life on the reservation.

6

WE MOVED TO A SMALL TOWN IN SOUTHERN OKLAHOMA
called Purcell and into Anna's house on Apache
Street. Shorty was confined to the back yard, and Princess
to a pasture five miles away.

My step-mother was a lady of rigid ideas and firm con-
victions. She set out to do an immediate make-over on me
before school started. I would be entering eighth grade in
junior high, she explained. It was a fresh start and an
opportunity for good impressions.

She stuffed my levis and overalls into a bag and shoved
them into the closet along with both pair of my cowboy
boots.

We went to Oklahoma City to buy material for new
dresses. Then to the seamstress who pushed and pinned,
prodding me with questions about Dad while she measured patterns to my shoulders.

Then, my step-mother took me shopping for a bra. I was
not a willing customer. I hated the very idea. I was as flat

chested at twelve as I had been at five. She laughed at my hesitation and told the sales lady "we" wanted to see the training bras. When I refused to even look, Anna chose two.

Before we'd left the farm, I bobbed my hair off just below my ears and wore it parted down the middle. I'd seen a picture of Geronimo and fashioned my style after his. Anna shuffled me immediately off to her beauty shop. "Let's do something," she told her beautician. "Anything."

Bub wrote me a letter describing boot camp and I decided life with Anna was similar to the Air Force. You were watched constantly, lectured frequently, and reprimanded harshly for your mistakes.

My heart ached for the farm. To run barefoot through the deep grass, swim in the creek, feel the freedom of the endless hills. The five miles that separated me from my horse seemed like two hundred. I wasn't allowed to walk out alone, and except for weekends, Dad didn't find time to drive me.

Shorty had to remain penned in the back yard. He spent his days walking the fence and whining. The sound of his unhappiness drove me insane. I'd let my dog out of the yard and start walking. But there was no place to get alone, no creek to play in, and no sense of freedom anywhere, so we often ended up hiding together in the back yard hedge.

Although Sis was living only a few hours away in Ponca City, she was married and busy with her new life. She seldom called. I'd written three letters to Bub's one and had haunted the mail box for weeks, but he wasn't good at answering. Lil Bub adapted more easily to city life. "David" and his new friends played baseball, walked down for snow-cones, and had sleep-overs.

By the time school started, my attitude was simple. I didn't like Purcell or anything about it. Maybe the white soldiers had captured me, hauled me off to the reservation, but they couldn't make me like it.

The long hallways and many turns in the Purcell school were confusing. Remembering where my locker was and the combination seemed an impossible task. I felt as though everyone watched me, talked about me all the time. I missed Shorty being by my feet, the old days at Braden School.

Anna insisted I take a Home Economics class and become part of the Future Homemakers of America. I went along in whichever direction she channeled me, because although Dad had become a silent partner in the parenting, he reinforced each of Anna's ideas.

Every time I'd see the flash of a blue and gold Future Farmers of America jacket, my heart would thump with nostalgia. If Dad hadn't married, if we hadn't moved, I'd have a calf to show or a hog or a sheep, I'd be in Future Farmers of America where I belonged.

Besides Shorty, books were still my closest companions. I absorbed all the stories I could find about Geronimo after he went to Fort Sill. How he adapted to prison life. With a growing sense of defeat, I did try to accept my new surroundings.

My filly grew into a flashy sorrel mare with light flaxen mane and tail. She was green broke, gentle natured, and she always nickered eagerly when she saw me approaching.

Sometimes Dad would be in a good mood and drop me off for the entire day. I'd take along a sandwich, an apple, and a canteen full of water. Shorty would follow me and Princess to the nearby banks of the Canadian River where we'd play away the hours.

The first serious problem with Anna arose from those days of freedom along the river. She decided that it wasn't proper for a young lady to meander along the river banks, unsupervised. When I begged, Dad did put in a few words in my behalf, but Anna wouldn't budge. Soon, even my days along the river were stolen away. The renegade rose up in me.

"As long as the grass grows and the water flows," I would say sometimes to my step-mother, in an Indian monotone. She had absolutely no idea what I meant.

When my freedom along the river was taken, I rebelled. One night after my little brother went to bed, I striped my face with red finger paint, took off my shirt and put on a pair of worn levis. I walked bare-footed into the front room. Dad and Anna were in their recliners watching television and laughing. I stood behind them for several moments in silence, hating their happiness.

When Dad finally saw me, he walked to the T.V. and clicked it off. Anna turned and gave out a little gasp.

"Want new treaty," I said, folding my arms. "Not happy here, no freedom on this reservation."

Dad kind of grinned at first, then he got a bewildered look and ran his fingers through his stubble hair.

"Sissy, what in hell's name are you doing?"

"Want new treaty," I repeated. "Want freedom to ride the river."

Dad continued to stare, wordless.

"Young Lady," Anna said, "I think you better go get your shirt on and get that paint cleaned off your face, please."

I stood, arms still folded, and stared straight ahead without moving.

Dad had reared back in his recliner and when I didn't move, his chair slammed down with a thump and he jumped out of it red-faced. "You do as you're told."

I walked back to my room, with him giving me little shoves. As soon as he left my bedroom, I crawled out the window into the back yard and hid in the hedge with Shorty.

A few days later, an old Indian man named Tyree, moved into a house on our street. Anna's friend, who lived across the street, prided herself in being the neighborhood lookout. She took personal responsibility to know, who, what, when, and where.

Together, she and Anna formed a quick negative opinion about Mr. Tyree.

At supper one night, Anna made an announcement. "That old Indian man that moved into the little house is crazy. I want you kids to stay clear away from that corner."

She might as well have mailed me a hand-written invitation. What an irresistible combination of characteristics, he was Indian and Anna didn't like him.

For days I watched the house, letting David's baseball roll close enough to peek or walking Shorty down the sidewalk. I listened carefully to tidbits of gossip. Stories about the old man clustered. He was an owl, never coming out during the day. He didn't have visitors or family. The mystery surrounding him seemed to blend nicely with Halloween and so I decided that night was the perfect time to make my move.

David was trick or treating with friends and Anna told me to go along with them. The three of them were embarrassed by my tagging after only one house. At the end of the block, I stopped and stared at the little corner house. It was the perfect opportunity.

"You guys just go wherever you want. Meet me back here in an hour."

David looked at Mr. Tyree's dark yard and then at me. He gave a suspicious frown. "What're you gonna do, Sissy."

"Shorty and I will just hang out, don't worry." I said.

As soon as the three bumped away with their paper bags, I looked down at Shorty. "Let's do it," I said, and he gave a little "Errf" of agreement.

I held my dog in my arms when I knocked at the door. Except for the full moon over my shoulder, everything was black. It was the only house on the block not lit and decorated for the festivities.

My first knock was feeble. I strained my ears for any stirrings from within. Nothing. The second knock was stronger, but still no reply. I took my fist then and banged the screen door until it slapped loudly against the frame.

Finally the door creaked open and a pair of cloudy brown eyes stared down at me. "What is it?" The voice barked.

"Trick or treat," I said, hoping to somehow get a good look at the old man.

"What? What's that you're sayin, girl?"

He spoke loud and with an impatient edge.

"You know," I said, swallowing my fear, "It's Halloween. Trick or Treat time."

I felt the uncertainty in his brown eyes as we stared. I began to explain. "It's a holiday, you know, like Christmas. All the kids dress up in scary costumes and go around to everyone's house and say, 'Trick or Treat.' People give them apples and candy and stuff."

"I have not candy, no apples," he said, shutting the door with a slam. But, before I could turn and leave the porch, the door cracked open again. "I would have some home-canned juice."

It was an invitation. I accepted with an eager nod. "I'd have to bring my dog. He goes everywhere with me."

The door opened wider and I stepped into the darkness.

When he pushed the door shut, I stood, rigid at first. What if the stories about him were true, if he were crazy? I pondered for a moment there in the darkness. I wasn't sure what that meant. Back on the farm one of the neighbor girls was retarded. People said she was crazy. She always ran out to the car when we drove in to visit. She hugged me tight and giggled with joy that I'd come. And she liked to play with the butterflies and was kind to the animals.

Mr. Tyree made a shuffling noise from the next room then a match raked across something rough and he lit a candle.

"Come on," he growled and motioned for me. He had a wooden table with two spoolbacked chairs. I sat down and strained my eyes to focus on anything through the dim light. Back in the front room the hardwood floor shined bare in the candlelight. I couldn't see one stick of furniture, a television, not even a chair. I wondered what he could do all day, alone inside the small house.

He sat two empty pint jars on the table, then reached on a shelf and brought down a full quart of dark juice. From his pocket, he took a rusty knife, and with shaking fingers, pried the golden lid off with a pop.

"Blackberry," he said. "Say when, whoa."

I watched silently as he filled my pint to the rim.

"Thirsty?"

I nodded eagerly, but it was a lie. I'd had a soda pop just before we left the house. I wanted a big glass so I could stay the full hour and visit.

"You Indian?" I asked, squirming with curiosity. He nodded and sat slowly in the chair across from me.

"You?" He hollered.

"Dad says no. Says I'm Scotch, Irish, and German, but I think he's wrong. Must have been an Indian somewhere in the wood pile cause I just *feel* Indian. Like I have the talk and spirit of them in the deepest part of my ownself."

He grinned and a gold tooth sparkled in the candlelight.

"Geronimo is my favorite." I continued, hoping he'd get into the conversation. When he didn't respond I continued. "For a long time he escaped the white soldiers and the reservation. Even when they captured him, they didn't kill his spirit."

"You know much about this Geronimo."

"I read a lot," I said.

We sat for a long time then in silence. I wanted to ask him what tribe he was and where he came from and a thousand other things, but decided it might be rude. I kept hoping he'd talk, but he seemed perfectly content to sit and sip his juice.

All of a sudden he stood, making his way across to the shelves above the sink. He came back carrying something.

"Checkers?" He asked.

I nodded and smiled.

We were on our second game, sitting in complete silence when the rattling knock sounded at the door. Mr. Tyree's bones popped when he stood, and he walked with a limp.

I heard my brother's voice come meekly through the screen.

"Sorry to bother you, Sir, but would my sister by any chance be here? She's taller than me with red-gold hair and has a spotted dog."

I stuck my head between Mr. Tyree and the door.

"Sissy, I been waitin and waitin. It's past nine, Anna will skin us."

I offered my hand to Mr. Tyree and he took it firmly. I'd

seen Dad thank people when he left from a visit. "Much obliged for the juice and the game."

He grunted and opened the screen door. "Come again, girl."

Shorty wiggled out of my arms the minute I walked out. He ran to a nearby tree and lifted his leg.

"What're we gonna tell Anna?" David asked as the three of us started off.

"Just say the time got away from us," I said, making it sound lots easier than I knew it would be. My mind was still humming from my visit with Mr. Tyree.

"What's he like?" David asked. "Does he really live without furniture or food or . . ."

"He's just an old man," I said, "who likes to play checkers."

Anna met us at the door and made us both sit at the table.

"Do you know what time it is?" I didn't, but opened my mouth with the excuse. She didn't allow it. "If you two can't meet curfew then maybe next time you just won't go."

David's eyes were on me. I knew I had to say something to take the blame from him. "Sorry," I said.

Temporarily satisfied, Anna sent us off for baths and bed.

As soon as the hall light went off and I heard Dad and Anna's bedroom door close, I unlatched the screen and slipped out into the back yard with my sleeping bag.

Usually I awoke when the sun first hit the eastern horizon. I'd shake the dry grass from my sleeping bag, roll it and stick it through the window, then crawl in and latch the screen before Anna's alarm clock sounded. But that morning, the telephone rang before the alarm and Anna came storming into my room and caught me in the yard.

"I thought we decided it wasn't a good idea to sleep in the yard." She said, hanging her head out my window and reaching to latch the screen.

I stood and began to shake the grass from my sleeping bag.

"You come on in right now, your Dad and I need to talk to you."

Anna was furiously fixing breakfast when I walked in the back door. She had bacon sizzling, coffee brewing, and was mixing pancakes. When she looked at me, I realized she was mad about something other than me sleeping outside. Her eyes were flashing with anger.

"Did I or did I not forbid you and David to go around that old Indian's house?"

Godfrey, Anna's lookout had somehow caught wind of my visit the night before. "You did," I said, without emotion.

"So what did you do at that house?" she asked, just as David and Dad took a seat at the table.

I sank down into a chair and glanced at David, who had a look of horror on his face. *How did she find out?* His eyes asked.

"Played checkers," I said, nonchalantly.

"Is that it?"

"Drank some home-canned fruit juice."

Anna let out a shriek and turned to Dad, slamming her fork down. "God, she'll probably die of Botulism."

It sounded like an Indian word to me, so I came to my own defense. "No, I'll be fine. I'm Indian and safe from their diseases."

Anna stared at me, like a calf looking at a new gate. "I think you've done and said enough. I don't want you to *ever* go in that old man's house again. You understand me?"

"Yes ma'am."

And I *didn't* go in the house again. But every chance I got when I knew Anna was at work or gone for an hour, I'd sneak into the back yard, through the hedge and onto Mr. Tyree's porch. His back yard was so hidden by trees that even the neighborhood snitch couldn't see through. I'd knock and when he'd see me, he'd hold up a bony finger, which meant he'd go after the checkers. We'd sit in the silence and play. Shorty would sleep by my feet, waking occasionally to snap at an irritating fly.

Often, I'd interrupt the silence with a question, yearning to know more about Mr. Tyree's past. But he either didn't hear well or preferred to not answer.

I'd stand when it was time for me to go. He'd flash his gold tooth. "Come again, girl."

One afternoon, Anna left work early and caught me playing checkers on Mr. Tyree's porch. That evening, at the supper table, she announced my punishment.

"You aren't to ride your horse for a month and if I catch you anywhere near that old man's house . . . it'll be two months off the horse."

I put my fork down slowly and stared at her until she made me leave the table. Princess and Mr. Tyree were all I had. Saturdays with my mare and a few secret checker games.

After the hall light went off and the bedroom door closed, I clicked on the flashlight and pulled a map from beneath my pillow. I found Ponca City and circled it with a red pen then ran a straight line from Purcell north through Oklahoma City up to my destination. It was about a hundred and fifty miles. I unlatched the screen and pulled my sleeping bag toward the hedge. It was late November and the nights were getting cool. I thought about the farm and how the leaves would be turning along the creek.

"We'll leave at first light," I told my friend.

Shorty sat in front of me and I daubed a jagged line down both sides of his face with paint, then did my own. I lifted my arms up to the half moon. "As long as the grass grows and the water flows," I sang, letting my voice rise and fall in rhythmic repetition.

Shorty lifted his head and howled.

7

THE MORNING AIR WAS BRISK WHEN I OPENED MY EYES. THE sound of clattering leaves pulled me back, to the blackjack trees, the creek, the freedom of the wind. My dog put his head on my shoulder and whined as I carried him.

In an hour we were across town, nearing the Canadian River bridge. Princess was less than a mile away. We stopped and hid behind some trees to rest. I dug a piece of jerky from my pack and shared it with Shorty, then we drank from my canteen. I took the map from my back pocket.

"We can ride along the Canadian, here," I showed Shorty, "until we get around Oklahoma City to the west. Then we'll cut up through here, hit the Cimarron, and go back west to Stillwater. From there the farm is less than twenty miles north east. We'll stick to the rivers so the trees will hide us." Shorty looked up at me while he panted. The whites of his eyes showed more than usual, as if his eyebrows were raised with interest. "What do you think?"

He gave an enthusiastic bark of approval.

Just as we came out of the bushes and started up on the bridge, I caught a glimpse of a familiar pickup, puttering toward us. We ducked back down, but too late. Dad's truck began to slow and he pulled off the road.

"Run," I yelled, leaping out of the brush I took off down under the bridge, across the wide stretch of sand. I had two choices, the bridge or the river. That time of year, the Canadian wasn't much more than a creek. I wasn't afraid to cross it. If I got caught on the bridge, I'd be trapped. Half way across the sand, I glanced to the other bank and my heart stopped. Red lights flashed on the other end of the bridge and one police car had pulled down a dirt road and was waiting near the sandy edge on the other bank.

"They called the cops," I said, outloud. Shorty barked.

"Don't worry, Buddy, they'll never catch us. Never."

Running fast, I sprinted back to the bank of the Canadian and started through the deep brush. When I'd run as far as I could, I slid down behind the trunk of a cottonwood and lifted my canteen. Shorty dropped beside me and spread out against the cool ground.

"Somehow, we'll have to get Princess later," I told Shorty. "For now we have to lose the cops." I poured a drink in the palm of my hand and Shorty lapped it up.

Then I heard the commotion behind us. Someone was coming through the weeds. Without hesitating, I took off in another dead run. Voices came up around me.

"There she is."

"Go to the east, John."

"Send a car down Red Hill to approach from the south."

With a snap decision, I decided to go back west, toward town. They were getting me in a corner. When I doubled back, I almost ran straight into a fat cop. A huge hand came out for me, but I dodged it and kept running.

"She's over here," his voice sounded through the walkie talkie in between gasps for breath.

Dropping down onto my knees and crawling, I found a culvert. I followed it and came out in an alley several blocks away from my pursuers. I had to put all the distance I could between us.

On the farm, running had been second nature to me. I ran everywhere and loved to race. I could outrun everyone. At the last day of school picnic I always won the footrace, even against the biggest boys.

Trying to stay near cover, I lit out with Shorty at my heels. When I reached the west end of Purcell my plans changed abruptly. I knew every cop in town would soon be right behind me. I'd head north instead of returning south east to Princess. If I could reach the highway I'd hitch us a ride and get out of Purcell, away from the immediate danger. Somehow, when things settled down, I'd return for my horse.

On the far north edge of town, when I could hear the distant buzz of traffic from the interstate, I saw another police car. He was driving slowly, looking. I hit the dirt and grabbed Shorty, holding him close to me. But I was too late. He'd caught a glimpse of me.

"Sighted the runaway, just south of the interstate, I'm leaving the car." The voice sounded clear over the radio.

I jumped to my feet and took off. Right in front of me was a brick wall that seemed to stretch forever around a huge building. I couldn't stop to consider my options. I could hear footsteps slamming against the pavement just behind me. An entrance inside the wall lay directly in front of me.

Shorty helped me make the decision by dashing toward the gates. We bounded across a green lawn where old people sat in wheel chairs. The minute I stopped to look, I knew I'd made a mistake. The wall stretched around the nursing home in a wide circle, with only one entry.

When I turned back to the entrance, I saw the same fat cop that had nearly grabbed me by the river. He was huffing toward us, sweat rolling down his face, soaking his uniform. I stood and waited until he was within six feet of me then I hollered and took off around him, barely escaping through the entrance before the big paw reached out.

"Damn it," I heard him swear.

Shorty and I made it around the fence and bolted off across a plowed field that bordered the highway. My breath was coming in short jerks and my face was burning. Just as I began to feel some relief, I heard a siren and then another. Police cars pulled along the highway on each side of the field. I looked back and saw the fat cop waddling up from behind.

Like a raccoon trapped by hounds, I did the only thing

I could, I tried first one way then another, with policemen reaching, grabbing, missing. I darted and spun and was finally on my knees crawling when two of them grabbed me with strong hands, gripping my arms.

Shorty dived and grabbed one of them by the ankle. The cop let out a squall and lost his grip on my shoulder. Just as Shorty went back in for another attack, I heard a familiar voice and looked up to see Dad.

"Settle down, boy," he had Shorty by the collar.

"She can run like a damn lizard on a flat rock, Jesus," the fat cop said, mopping his face with a handkerchief.

Dad took Shorty in the truck with him. The fat cop and Dad argued for awhile about something, then Dad drove away and the cop made me ride with him in the front seat of his car to the police station.

"Young lady, you've done a serious thing here today. Do you know that?"

I squinted at him with a straight stare and could see my war stripes on my cheeks.

"We could put you in juvenile detention for this. Or your Dad could send you off to reform school. You couldn't make it on your own, you know. You'd starve or end up on the streets."

The whole time he ranted, I kept thinking of Geronimo, how he must have felt that first time they captured him and forced him on the reservation.

The sergeant lectured me for at least forty-five minutes. In the car, into the station, past the front desk, back to his office. Threatening. Bringing up examples of other teens who'd been murdered along Interstate 35.

"What do you have to say, young lady? I'm sure you're real sorry now for what you've done, now aren't you? A pretty young gal like you, well I'll bet you're ready to go home and behave."

"Awooney Bawla Caw," I said, in a curse, then jumping to my feet I added, "Soma Sina Woochoo."

I started out the door and ran smack into Dad. The fat cop came right behind me, raving. "You've got a real problem, Mr. Jacobs. She's a damn renegade. Prison material. You better do yourself a favor and put her somewhere right now, while you still can."

Dad's face turned red. "I'll decide what's best and I don't need your opinion."

"Fine," the fat cop hollered as we started out the door. "Tell your wife not to call us next time. I'm not chasing that little brat half way across the county again."

Dad drove straight home without saying one word. When we went into the house, Anna started in. Before she got two words out I raised my hand.

"Shorty and I have made up our minds, we're not stayin. Either I'll call Mama and see if I can live with her, or . . . I'll keep runnin away. You can't stop me."

Dad let out a tired sigh. "She means it," he said to Anna. "We might just as well let her go live with her mother. At least that way I'll know where she is."

Anna's mouth kind of fell shut and she got a perplexed look on her face.

Dad looked down at me. "Go in and call your mother.

See if she'll come get you."

Mama's last letter was in my dresser drawer. I pulled it out and sat on the bed. She'd written a couple of months before and sent me a telephone number. Her an Hank were still living in Ponca City in a small apartment. But if I ever wanted to come live with them, she'd try to find an acreage in the country so I could bring Shorty and Princess.

Dad walked in and sat next to me on the bed. "Sissy," he said, "you're just going from the skillet into the fire." He ran thick fingers through his stubble hair. "I'm looking at a farm right now south of Purcell. I know you and Shorty hate being in town. Eventually, Anna and I will build a new home out in the country."

It was at least an effort and I appreciated it. For one moment, my heart tugged with regret. Leaving Dad wasn't going to be so easy. But, "eventually" sounded like an eternity to me.

I waited, aching for Dad to say more. Tell me things would be different. That I could have my horse no matter what. That he'd find a farm soon, very soon. We sat in silence for a few minutes, then he stood and walked out of the room.

My fingers grasped the telephone until my knuckles turned white. I thought about David. Leaving him would be even harder. "Hank's been transferred to Newkirk, north of Ponca City. We've rented a place in the country."

When I hung up the phone, I felt some relief from the pain throbbing in my throat. The country. Shorty,

Princess, and I would be free.

I walked out into the front room and faced Dad. "She's comin for me late this evenin. I'll be goin to school in Newkirk."

Anna was crying. For a moment, I felt different toward her. She'd done a lot of nice things for me.

David had been crying when he came into the room.

"I want to go with Sissy," he said to Dad.

"You can't," Dad said, flatly. "I have complete custody of you kids until you're twelve and then you can decide for yourself."

The only sound at the table that evening was forks scraping against plates. My bags stood packed in a clump in the hallway.

In the middle of a long silence, someone knocked at the door with a rattling slam that vibrated the windows. All of us jumped.

When Dad pulled the door open, I heard the familiar barking voice. "Where's that girl?" Mr. Tyree squalled.

Dad got an embarrassed look on his face. He stuck out his hand. "I'm Dean Jacobs. You must be Mr. Tyree."

"Yes Sir," the old man grunted, "Nice to meet ya. Your Mrs. was by the house yesterday or day before. She acted mad because that girl was playin checkers with me." He was yelling, his words filling the house like blasts from a blow torch.

Dad shifted his weight from one foot to the other. "Well Sir, I . . ." He turned to Anna with a helpless look.

"Where's that girl?" Mr. Tyree demanded.

I slipped out of my chair and squeezed between Dad and the door. "Mr. Tyree, I'm movin. Goin to live with my Mama. I won't be around much anymore."

He blinked his cloudy eyes as if he didn't hear or couldn't quite comprehend. "You'll be on over to play checkers then?" He asked, squeezing my hand.

I got a lump in my throat, but nodded because I had no idea what else to say. A horn honked from the drive and I caught a glimpse of Mama's old station wagon.

When Shorty and I drove away, Mr. Tyree was making his way back toward his little house in confusion.

8

FINALLY, WE TURNED ONTO THE GRAVEL ROAD AND I SAW the house nestled in the cottonwood trees, my breath caught in my throat. The leaves along the lane were brilliant gold in the sunset and off through the thickness of brush I caught a sparkle of water.

"There's a creek?" Shorty jumped up in the seat and looked through the front glass.

"And a couple of good bass ponds," Mama said, "you're gonna love it here, Sissy."

The minute the station wagon rolled to a stop, Shorty and I bounded out. I tore off my shoes and socks and went crashing down toward the winding creek. Both of us splashed in. Shorty ran round and round yipping and I fell backward and went beneath the surface, letting the cool water drench my hair and clothes.

Then both of us crawled out and lay looking up at the sun shadowing through the autumn leaves.

"We'll sleep out here tonight, boy. No sirens screamin. In the silence, we'll watch the stars through the trees."

Shorty was too excited to lay still. He barked out a quick agreement, then bounded off after a jack rabbit that meandered along the path. He gave out little yeps of pleasure as he ran. He'd never caught a rabbit in his life, but he sure missed chasing them.

"Think you'll like it here?" Hank's voice was soft with gentleness. He sat on the bank beside me.

I nodded. Hank had always been nice enough, but I resented him. I pondered the complexity of that feeling. It was similar to what I felt toward Anna.

"It's pretty cool for swimming," he said, looking at my dripping clothes. "Is the water cold?"

"Not much. Shorty and I have just missed it so."

From day one, life in Newkirk was too good to be true. Everything seemed as though it had been waiting for us. The kids were all in 4-H and F. F. A., country kids who liked riding horses and fishing. Within a month Mama arranged to have Princess hauled to Newkirk. I had my dog, my horse, and a new life.

In school I joined the basketball team, became a member of the yearbook staff and by the end of first semester, was in the National Honor Society.

By the following spring, I had a room full of ribbons. My best friend, Terry Sparks, lived just across the state line in Kansas. Every afternoon I'd jump on Princess and Shorty and I would go two miles to meet her then we'd ride until dark. On weekends I'd ride Princess to the rodeo grounds near the state line where Terry and I competed in barrel racing, pole bending, and other events at the rodeos. My dog roamed the rodeo grounds for choice tidbits and visited with people.

That year, I began to wear a bra. Instead of shirtless Indian ceremonies, I started writing down my passion and pain, spilling my yearnings onto one blank page after another. Early mornings, at lunch, after school, I kept a running inventory of my daily life.

The Native American connection, however, did not end. Every evening I had a special writing ritual with Shorty, near the creek. With my penny and a crumpled textbook picture of Geronimo, we'd build a small fire and seek the peace.

On one such evening, as I sat cross-legged by my fire, Mr. Tyree's face came before me and I felt a strong sense of sadness. David, who'd promised to look after my old friend, called the next morning. Mr. Tyree had died the night before in his sleep.

When Dad and Anna began to search for next of kin, they finally located a daughter out in California. She hadn't contacted the old man for many years.

I knew then why Mr. Tyree and I had instantly connected in friendship. And I truly believed he had come in his spirit journey to tell me, good-bye.

Shorty fell back into his old wandering habit and soon all the nearby neighbors knew his name. Usually, if he did go traveling, he'd return the next day.

Then one Saturday evening, he disappeared and I immediately got an uneasy feeling. Down to the barn, around the creek, out to the ponds I walked with the flashlight. It was April and he sometimes went out late chasing field mice beneath the moonlight. I called and called, but no answer. When I went to bed that night, I dreamed that Shorty was moving away from me. I was chasing him and he was crying, but he kept fading in the distance.

"He's probably just wandering, you know how he is," Mama said the next morning.

"But my dream had been too close to reality. I knew in the deepest part of me my dog was in trouble. But along with that feeling came the certain knowledge that he was still alive. I began a relentless search.

Each afternoon, I'd rush in from school change into levis and boots, and saddle up Princess. In the next few weeks I rode a twenty mile radius around our place asking all the neighbors.

With some of the money I'd made checking our land-lord's cows, I ran an ad in the Newkirk and Arkansas City papers. No response. April slid into May and I continued—checking all the culverts, under buildings, places I knew my Shorty could squeeze in pursuit of a rabbit.

One Sunday morning, I arose early and began to make myself a sack lunch before I began my search.

"Sissy," Mama said, "I know how much Shorty meant to you. But it's time to give this up. Your little dog is gone."

Her words brought me no grief, because I knew she was wrong. "He's not dead, Mama. I'd know."

Two and a half months later, on a golden July morning, Terry and I were riding through an alfalfa field several miles west of her house, still searching for my dog. When I heard the first little, "Errf" I stopped Princess dead still, listening. I saw the flash of brown and white spots come popping then disappearing through the thick alfalfa. I bailed off of Princess and began to run.

Shorty dived into my arms, barking, then bounded in tight circles around me, ecstatic with happiness. We rolled and laughed and cried in the sweetness of the field, then Terry helped me haul him up on the saddle and start home.

Mama shook her head in disbelief that afternoon when I walked down the road with Shorty in front of me on the saddle. "He sure is thin, I'll scramble him up some eggs and milk."

Shorty told me everything as we cuddled on the pillow that night. He'd been baited in back of a pickup by some coon hunters and taken far far away. For the last two and a half months he'd been traveling back to me. I listened and held him tight, realizing how close I'd come to losing the most important thing in my life.

Late that fall, in November, I stepped off the bus one afternoon and Shorty met me, like always, at the end of the gravel road. But on that day he acted strange. He ran up the drive, sat down and barked, then ran farther, like he wanted me to hurry. I bounded after him, books clattering.

When I walked into the house, I stood, shocked. Everything in the house was gone. Furniture, curtains, dishes. All that remained was my packed suitcases and Hank's stuff piled in a clump in the middle of the living room floor. I walked numbly through the house with Shorty beside me. He sat down in the bedroom and let out a lingering whine.

When I heard the old screen door slam, I ran toward the kitchen, hoping to see Mama, wanting to believe there was some sane reason for the house being empty.

Hank stood, shoulders slumped, his face pale. One look at him told me everything I needed to know. Mama had pulled her famous disappearing act. My step-dad walked through the house, bewildered, then he walked outside and sank down at the picnic table.

Shorty and I joined him, sitting for a long time before breaking the silence.

"You know where she went?" I asked, still hoping.

Hank shook his head. "I had a feeling it was coming. She's been getting . . . restless. She can only be satisfied in one place for so long." He said the words without a trace of anger, like he was talking about a naughty child.

"What . . . what will we do?" I asked, afraid of the answer.

"Sissy, you know I'd let you stay with me . . . but your Dad wouldn't hear of it." He hesitated. "I guess I'll get an apartment in town. You and Shorty and Princess will have to go back to Purcell."

I stared out across the rented farm and my eyes went blurry. With a dry gulp, I realized that the freedom of being in the country had given me my life back. Burning with the reality of returning to Purcell, I remembered what Dad said about going from the skillet into the fire.

"Back to the reservation," I mumbled.

Shorty nudged under my hand and crawled into my lap.

I took him into my arms. "That's true, buddy, at least we're goin together."

9

SHORTY CONTINUED WITH ME ON MY JOURNEY TOWARD young adulthood. We returned to Purcell for part of one school year, then when Mama bought a small place on the river in Osage County, we moved back to Ponca City.

By then, Mama's drinking controlled her life. She had divorced Hank and was working swing shift at a beer joint in Ponca. Sometimes she didn't come home for days. When she did, she was either bouncy and fun or drunk and disagreeable.

Life with Mama was never dull. I could depend on her undependability. If anything at school was important to me, she wouldn't show up. For holidays, birthdays, and other such events, she'd often build you up for days, talking about what "we" were going to do, then disappear completely or show up so smashed you were ashamed to claim her.

On the other hand, Mama had a magical child-like side that was irresistible. Sometimes she'd be home in the mornings, singing from the kitchen. I'd awake to the smell of bacon and blueberry pancakes. She'd serve me breakfast in bed, ask me all about school and listen intently.

She'd tell of a time in her school days when she used to walk down the halls mocking the stiff-kneed Principal. Striding across my bedroom floor with a hysterical expression, she'd limp and swing her body in a half circle until I'd fall back into my pillow, giggling.

I turned sixteen, a junior in high school that year on the Arkansas River with Mama. Shorty was pushing eleven years old. When his muzzle grayed and his hearing faded, a nagging fear began to haunt me.

We were living only five miles from the old farm, so I was back near the kids I'd gone to school with at Braden. I tried to rekindle some of my friendships, but soon found that years of change cut deep canyons of distance.

Most of the girls I'd grown up with were either pregnant and had quit school or were planning to marry as soon as they graduated. Measured in terms of hormones, they were light years ahead of me. I still preferred riding horses and fishing on the river, alone.

And that year, 1965, was the beginning of a solo lifestyle that became second nature to me. The river house was little more than a shack, with lopsided floors and cracks that the wind whistled through. Two days after Shorty and I arrived, we named it the Mouse House. Mice were everywhere. In the cupboards, under the beds and furniture. At night, they scampered and chewed and squeaked.

Sometimes I'd awake in the night to a commotion when Shorty would attack one of the intruders who was trying to join us under the covers. In the wee hours of the morning I'd feel my dog stand and stiffen on the bed. After a moment of silent concentration, he'd hit the cold linoleum floor running. Catching the squeakers off guard, he'd snap viciously, slinging them over his shoulder until the floors in the small house resembled the Battle of Gettysburg.

I don't know who was more amusing, Shorty, with his passion for annihilating the endless supply of rodents, or Mama. She'd come in half-drunk sometimes at night and declare war on the mice. With a handful of steel wool, she'd sit and stuff cracks and holes for hours. She'd set traps with chocolate, peanut butter, and cheese temptations. And think out loud as she worked.

"You little thieves. You think you can take over, do you? Well you can't outsmart me. No sir. I'll stuff every crack, every hole in this house if it takes me from now until forever."

In many ways the Mouse House holds fond memories for me. Shorty had a chair at the table where he ate off of his own plate when Mama wasn't around. He slept on my pillow each night. In warm weather I took the screen off of my window and Princess often rested her head inside on the foot of my bed. On weekends, the three of us slept on the banks of the Arkansas River, camped beneath the stars next to a crackling campfire.

We lived sometimes on catfish, froglegs, and ate wild poke, with blackberries and persimmons for dessert. Other times Mama would come in with bags of wonderful groceries, cook pot roast, bake cookies and bread. Lingering smells of yeast, sugar, and browned beef would liven up the Mouse House for days.

Usually when Mama arrived drunk, she'd sleep off her booze then be fairly civil for a day or two. But there were times, and they became more frequent, when she was unreasonable and obnoxious.

One afternoon, I had just settled down, with Shorty in my lap, to finish a term paper for my English class when I heard the old station wagon rattle up into the yard. Mama rarely came in that time of the afternoon. Probably she'd been drinking.

"What cha, doin?" She asked, walking in and standing over me. She had a cocky tone to her voice that told me she was just itching for a good fight.

I knew immediately she was drunk and I felt a sense of dread settle over me like a fog. Mama loved to fight when she was drinking. I don't know whether it was something in her Irish blood, or just a chemical reaction to the booze, but on that day, I knew what was coming. I avoided confrontations with her at every turn. The last thing I wanted was to leave the river. I had my dog and my horse and school, the three things that were most important to me.

"Shorty and I are workin on a term paper that's due tomorrow."

"Well, why don't we go in to town to Chick and Millie's,

get some ribs. I juss got paid. Come on, what do you say?"

The image of Chick and Millie ribs brought saliva to my mouth. The crisp curly french fries and Texas toast.

"I'd like to, but when are you comin back. I have to finish this paper tonight and it's gonna take me awhile."

"Oh, come on," she said, "We'll be right back."

I looked at Shorty. His black eyes were locked on me with intensity. *You're setting yourself up again,* he said, but I ignored the reality.

"Come on, buddy, let's go. Wouldn't you like some of those nice rib bones?" As I walked toward the door, Shorty stopped and sat on the porch.

"Errff," he said, impatiently.

"Oh, come on," I coaxed him into the car, whispering, "it'll be different this time, wait and see." But I knew, deep in my soul, Shorty was right. I hated myself for always giving Mama second chances.

Interacting with my mother was like running barefoot through a thicket of sandburs. You might have a slim chance of getting to the other side unharmed, but the odds were discouraging.

We drove five miles in virtual silence and when we approached town, Mama pulled off in front of the 77 Club.

I gave her a squinted stare. She knew how I felt about sitting in the car while she went into the beer joint to drink beer.

"Red's car is here, I'm just going in for a minute," she said, in a patronizing voice.

"Mama," I said, when she put her hand on the door.

"I've served my time in front of beer joints waitin for you to come out. I will not sit here for long."

She gave me a despicable look. I knew I'd just set myself up, and with a sigh of exhaustion, I also knew at that moment, Shorty and I'd probably be walking the nine miles back home, hungry.

Fifteen minutes later Shorty scratched the door and barked. "Go ahead, say I told you so."

We walked into the bar. Ma was sitting with two guys in a booth, with double bottles of beer backed up. When she saw me, she grinned.

"Here's my kid," she said, grabbing me by the arm. "This is Red. Sit down for a minute. We'll go eat pretty soon."

I stared at her with a squint. I knew all about Mama's "pretty soons." They ranged anywhere from five hours to four days. "Mama, if we aren't gonna go eat, I'm walkin home."

"Smart mouth kids," She said. "They always know more than you."

I'd been suckered into her trap. I hated myself for taking the bait. Shorty took a few steps toward the door.

"Errff."

It was after dark that evening when we finally made it home. I slumped down onto the porch, tired and hungry and began to cry. Shorty collapsed next to me, licking his blistered feet.

"I won't trust her again. I promise, buddy. You're right, it's never gonna change."

Shorty crawled into my lap and licked my face. He said he understood my need to believe her, but it was time for me to accept the reality that I couldn't help Mama.

I spent the rest of the night finishing my term paper, sleeping about two hours before school.

Mama didn't return home for two weeks after that incident. When she did, she began packing her assortment of suitcases and boxes. She came in drunk, cursing her boss, saying the bill collectors were cheating her. All the world was against her.

"We're getting out of this God-forsaken state, going to Texas. Get busy and pack. Things will be different in Texas, Sissy. Hank's there. I called him and we've talked. He has a nice place near a lake . . ."

Shorty nudged up under my hand and looked at me, with a reminding stare as I sat, eating an apple. I knew he was right. Things with Mama were never going to be different. It was time for me to accept the overwhelming truth of that.

Suddenly she stopped and stared. "I told you to start packing."

"Shorty and I aren't goin, Mama. You do what you have to do. We'll do what we have to."

"You mean go back to Purcell," she threatened, knowing my weakness.

"Well, maybe we will," I said, swallowing to contain the fear in my voice.

An hour later, Mama thumped out of the drive with her old station wagon stuffed to the ceiling.

"Tell Anna hello," she called, waving as she drove off.

Shorty jumped out of my lap and started down toward the river, barking. I quickly bridled Princess, jumped on her back and followed him. He led me into the coolness of the Arkansas River, where my tears were washed away by the muddy water.

A few days after Mama left, a country preacher and his wife stopped by to pay a visit. They were new in the community and wanted to meet all the neighbors.

I was nervous when I invited them to sit at the picnic table and offered them a glass of ice water. The only time in my life I'd been around church people was at Grandma Carrie's in Purcell. Sometimes I went to her church and sat for hours on the hard pew listening to the angry preacher scream words that brought fear into my heart. When I tried reading from the Bible, I had more questions than answers.

But driven by the terror of Shorty's immortality, I ceased the opportunity to ask someone more knowledgeable of such things. The preacher looked at me intently across the table beneath shaggy dark brows.

"Do you go to church, young lady?"

I cleared my throat as Shorty settled near my feet. "No sir, not much." I squirmed uncomfortably for a moment then the question burst out of my mouth. "Do you think dogs go to heaven?"

The preacher's wife laughed. Then with a patronizing voice said, "Dogs don't have souls, child."

I looked at the preacher, hoping for a different answer.

When it didn't come, I picked up my old dog, stood and walked away, leaving my guests at the splintered picnic table.

At the river's edge I painted my face with pokeberry juice and stained Shorty's cheeks. I cried out my worry and fear with yearning squalls of despair.

"Awooney Bawla Caw? Soma Sina Woo Choo." A peaceful answer filtered slowly over me. My dog would travel beside me through the spirit world.

10

SHORTY AND I MANAGED ON OUR OWN AT THE MOUSE House for awhile longer. When the Landlord came to gather rent, I lied, telling him Ma was in the hospital. I gave him such a story, he kindly offered to loan me money before he left. Shorty and I devoured the last of the fried potatoes and cornbread that night.

A few days later, Sis and Gene came by to check on me, as they often did.

"Why don't you move in with us. Finish your senior year in Ponca. I'll talk to Dad." Sis said.

"We've got two acres," Gene said, "enough room for your animals. And we go fishing every weekend."

The offer sent my heart soaring. The small amount of money I made raising rabbits wasn't enough to live on and I knew I couldn't keep the Landlord fooled forever. Sis and I got along fine and Gene was fun to be around. Dad agreed with the arrangement, saying he'd send a little money to help with my school.

For my senior year, I took a job after school with Ray Lessert, the local veterinarian. I loved working with the animals and began to consider a career as a vet. By then, everyone had begun to ask, "What will you do after you graduate?"

Shorty and I discussed it at length. I had some motivation toward writing, but it was vague. Shorty finally convinced me to just continue with school. It didn't matter so much which direction we took, as long as we continued. School, after all, had been the one secure thing in our lives.

In June, 1966, I graduated from Ponca City High School and sent my transcript to Oklahoma State University, Dad's alma mater. He'd graduated from what was then Oklahoma Agricultural and Mechanical College in 1939, getting his Bachelor's Degree in Agriculture.

In August I received the news that I'd won a working scholarship to Murray Hall on campus, my room and board in exchange for work in the cafeteria. Along with that good news, came a dilemma. Dogs were not allowed in the dorms.

At first, I conceived the notion of sneaking my old friend in, but quickly dismissed that when I visited Murray and the stern-faced House Mother met me at the outside door, rule book in hand. After a lot of maneuvering, I found a friend of a friend who had an apartment off campus. She agreed to board my dog in her back yard so I could visit him every day.

Dad and Anna had built a new brick home on their farm south of Purcell by then. In the process of moving from Sis's house and getting ready for school, I left Shorty at Dad's for a few days while I got settled into my dorm room.

Shorty remembered Dad. That first afternoon, he jumped up on Dad's leg, then bounced along behind as my father went to feed his cows. When Dad relaxed in his wicker rocker on the patio, with a jug of iced tea, Shorty stretched out on the cool cement behind the rocker, like he was home.

When it was time for me to move my first load of things to the campus, I explained to Shorty I'd return in a few days for him.

"I'll be back," I told him, kneeling and taking him in my arms. "Then we'll both get all settled in at our new school."

Shorty gave his little "Errff" and licked my hand.

"What did he say?" Dad asked, with a wry grin.

"Said he'd be here."

The following weekend I returned for my dog. After a leisurely Sunday dinner with Dad and Anna on the patio, I walked out to say good-bye to Princess. I put my arms around her neck and stood for several moments while she rustled her lips across my hair.

"You'll have it made here, old girl. Knee-deep grass and no one throwing a hot saddle on you." I gave her one last kiss on the velvet nose and turned to walk away. She nickered and followed me to the gate. When I reached the yard, I looked back at her and a flood of memories washed over me. The thrill of seeing her that first day, standing wide-eyed and weak-kneed at Maybelle's side. The times we ran naked and carefree across the hills, painted with poke-berry juice. Swimming the Arkansas River behind the Mouse House.

"She'll be just fine," Dad said, coming up behind me.

I used my sleeve to smother my emotion then walked over to get Shorty from his place behind the rocker. When I bent to pick him up, he growled at me. I stood up and stared down at him, crushed.

"Guess I woke him from his nap," I said, embarrassed. When I tried the second time, his growl deepened into a serious warning.

I gave a nervous laugh, looking at Dad then back down at my dog. "Come on fella, its time to go to school. We've made it from Braden to a genuine University. We can't quit now."

His cloudy eyes were intense as I knelt to talk to him. When I started to lift him, he actually snapped at me.

"He's always been a smart one," Dad said, rubbing his chin. "I think he wants to retire on the farm, Sissy. His edu-cation is over."

"What?" I asked, bewildered. "But he has to go, I mean we've always studied together."

"He's been talking to you since you were five years old," Dad said, "you can't stop listening to him now."

Shorty barked twice, agreeing with Dad, then he jumped up and snuggled against my neck for a brief moment. "You really want to stay here?" I choked.

My old dog went behind the rocker and stretched out, plopping his gray muzzle on his paws.

"I know how much he means to you, Sissy," Dad said, and for the first time, I noticed all the silver streaking his red hair.

"I'll take good care of him."

Nodding, I took one step, stopped and turned. I had an urge to yank my old friend up and take him against his will. He was getting senile and didn't understand what was happening. But the cloudy eyes were talking with vivid clarity.

You have to take this step without me, he said, begging me to allow him the choice. *The time to say good-bye is now.*

I knew he was thinking of me. College was going to be difficult and I needed to concentrate all my efforts on studying. Shorty had made a very adult decision. And he handled it with a lot more dignity than I could manage.

I stumbled to the car and into my adult life.

The Last

I**N OKLAHOMA THERE'S A SAYING—IF A PERSON IS LUCKY,** he'll have one true love in his lifetime, one good pickup truck, and one loyal dog. Throughout my adult life, I was fortunate enough to have several loyal dogs, but none of them touched the tender places of my heart the way Shorty had. I couldn't allow that to happen, because I wasn't sure I could survive the outcome.

Then in 1993, twenty years after Shorty died, Jake came into my life. The German Shorthair was already on our ranch, in his kennel the first time I saw him. When we stared at each other through the wire pen, his honey-brown eyes held me, hypnotized.

"Finally found me a dog," my new husband said, walking up. "He's two years old and from a great line of bird dogs. Name's Jake."

I nodded and tried to pull my attention away from the dog, but when he scratched the gate and whined I kept staring.

"Let's keep him penned for awhile," Williams said. "Something wrong?"

His question didn't interrupt the memory.

I was seven. It was the winter of 1955. I lay huddled beneath the willow tree hugging Shorty dog. He was whining and I was humming, but I could still hear Mama and Dad arguing from the house.

"What is it, Okie?" My husband touched my arm.

I pulled away from him. "Nothing, Williams."

"You mean nothing you want to share with me," he said.

We were still using fond nicknames for each other, but the tension between us had become serious.

It was April. The deep snows melted and flashed across our ranch, blushing the meadows with Indian Paintbrush. One Sunday morning when Williams left for church, I hiked into the foothills of the nearby Uintah Mountains.

High atop a ridge, where the snow was still knee-deep, I sat on a fallen log in silence, wondering about the purpose of my life. Unable to meet the necessary grade-point requirements for pre-vet med, I dropped out of college. When Shorty died, I sold my first article to a magazine called *The National Humane Review*. "The Decision" was a story about saying good-bye to my oldest and dearest friend.

After twenty years of grueling hard work as a professional freelance writer, I had fifty magazine articles in print, and boxes of unsold novels. I'd made a grand total of $20,000. A ridiculous average of $1,000 a year! At forty-four, I'd recently entered my third marriage and was already unhappy.

My new husband had a link to God that created a growing restlessness in me. Many times since Shorty's death, I'd tried to connect to a Supreme Being. In the deepest part of me, I yearned to have peace of mind, to feel like my life wasn't just a long series of mistakes.

So much heartache. So many unhealed wounds.

In August, 1982, Dad was killed on his farm near Purcell when his tractor flipped over and crushed him. He left a lot of words unspoken. We all did. By 1984, both of my beloved brothers were in different state prisons. Sis had been married and divorced four times. Mama was still drinking.

Where is God in all of that? I thought, standing and kicking at the snow.

When I returned to the barn that morning, Jake was sitting inside his kennel, head ducked, brown eyes intense. *Why can't I go?* he asked, with his eyes. Then he began to whine, politely, one little whimper then another. He took a big paw and scratched on his gate.

"It's okay, Shorty, you'll be okay, fella." I said without thinking. The slip caused my mind to plummet back to the spring of my ninth year, 1957.

"Do you know what divorce' means?" I asked, pulling Shorty into my lap.

Sis and Bub stared at each other, wordless, then they climbed quickly out of our hide-out and took off running fast across the field. I watched until their specks disappeared into the blackjack trees. Shorty started to whine, and scratched at my leg. I took him in my arms and held him tight. "It's okay, Shorty. You'll be okay, fella."

I turned and walked away from Jake's pen. "You aren't my dog or my responsibility," I called, kicking a bucket out of the way. "And the past is past."

A week later, Williams purchased a new four-wheel-drive All-Terrain Vehicle. Soon I was using it daily to check on the mares and foals in the far pasture. Every afternoon when I'd go to the hay barn to start the machine, Jake would watch me with quiet persistence. Tail flicking, sitting like a perfect gentleman, he'd beg me with his eyes.

For weeks I walked around Jake's kennel, ignoring him. But the love in his eyes, the patient way he sat, day after day, quietly begging, finally broke down my resistance.

"Well," my husband said, when I approached him one morning about exercising Jake. "Running would sure get him in shape for pheasant hunting."

I hesitated that first afternoon before I entered Jake's pen. What if he took off and didn't return?

"Now Jake," I told him, "you must stay near me and mind." His stub tail flicked patiently and his eyes sparkled toward the open gate behind me and the four-wheeler idling just outside.

His expression was that of a small child, his large feet shifted restlessly. I swallowed. It was a matter of taking the risk or walking past him every day, looking into those eyes.

We took off, he bounded obediently beside the four-wheeler, ecstatic with his freedom. We went down the gravel trail and turned off into the east meadow where mares grazed contentedly with new foals.

I stopped the machine and decided to walk with Jake to the stream. He dived into the cold water, dipping and splashing, then turned to me and whined. His whine took me to another creek on a summer day in 1958, when I was ten.

"Sissy, what're we gonna do?" My baby brother splashed his feet in the creek and pouted. Freckles stood out on his face like apple seeds across snow. "I love my daddy most the best of anything in this world, but we can't let Mama go drivin off by her ownself." He wiped angrily at his eyes. "Who're you gonna choose?"

I took Shorty up tighter in my arms. He slid under my chin and snuggled. "Shorty hasn't decided yet."

"Jake, come," I said, forcing the memory out of my mind. Immediately the proud head bounced up and he bounded out of the creek, dripping into my lap. He knocked me over, soaking me with muddy slop. I was on the ground, giggling and rolling like a kid. He licked my face and neck with foamy slurps. I crawled to escape, he darted out and back, eager to understand the rules of the new game. Finally, I managed to get on my feet and scold.

"Down, you . . . you . . . Big Goof." I changed my voice to mock my husband's deeper tone, "You can't get out of control here."

He sat, shoulders slumped. In dramatic, super slow motion he raised his eyes to me in question, then dropped them in shame. I burst out laughing. He jumped up, relieved that the mood had lightened.

When Jake ran into his kennel, he thanked me with a sloppy lick to my hand. The love in his eyes begged, *Hold me.*

My fingers trembled as I walked out and locked the gate.

That night, I had nightmares that jolted me awake and left my heart pounding. In the middle of the night, I jumped from bed and went into my study. Rummaging through the bottom of my file cabinet, I retrieved a small cedar box. I opened it and fingered the tarnished Indianhead penny, as I stared in disbelief at a faded photograph of Shorty . Looking back into those eyes, I could see they were Jake's eyes. And even though Shorty was much smaller than Jake, their brown spots were almost identical. I feared I was losing my mind.

The next morning June 22, 1993, I helped break thirteen yearlings to the flat saddle. That afternoon, when I started off on the four-wheeler with Jake, I was exhausted from the day's work and the previous sleepless night.

We left with a zoom. First gear, second, third, full

throttle. Jake's powerful feet kicked small gravel into the air and his floppy ears extended like wings in the wind.

As I turned off the road into our north pasture and headed down the dirt path, I remembered. Williams had given me a message for the hired hands. I pulled off the main trail. Dodging sagebrush and boulders, I began to climb. Juan and José were probably irrigating on the southeast end of the ranch. I'd take a short-cut. When I glanced over my shoulder I felt a tug of apprehension. From that elevation, the huge barns looked like monopoly-game houses, and the horses tiny dots.

Less than ten feet from the top of the mountain, the four- wheeler powered out. I felt the machine lug and tried shifting to a lower gear. It sputtered and I found myself stopped in a precarious position. I grabbed the brake and sat motionless for a moment. Gently, I began to release it and turn the wheels in an effort to start back down.

The four-wheeler tipped on two wheels and flipped, crashing over on top of me. Crushed into the rocks, face down, I struggled. Squirming and pulling my weight with my elbows, I tried snaking my way out. The back wheel was on my right hip and my left leg was bent up behind me. Five hundred pounds rested on my legs. The machine held me in a deadly vice.

Desperately, I reached and pulled rocks toward me, trying to wedge them between the wheel and the ground. My left ankle throbbed, threatening to explode. With one excruciating push up, I raised my back, held my weight on a shaking arm and jammed a rock under the wheel.

First came a moment of relief then the machine tilted. For one horrible second, it teetered above me, threatening to flip again, to crush my head and lungs. Then it slammed back on my legs. I let out a cry and rested my head against the rocks.

No one knew where I was. Williams wouldn't miss me until dark.

Jake came immediately to me. He whined when I moaned. He tried crawling under the machine as if he wanted to lift it away. He licked my face and flopped down on the flat rocks with his head a few inches from mine.

"Big Goof," I said, gritting my teeth against the biting agony, "look what I've gotten myself into." He crawled closer and put his chin on my head. Pulling off my leather glove, I commanded him to "Kennel." I had to hope someone would see Jake returning to the barn alone.

He knew the command. He let out a cry, took the glove and dashed down the mountain. About fifty feet away he stopped, looked back at me and with a look of turmoil, returned. I tried several times. He repeated the same pattern. He knew he should obey but he couldn't leave me.

In the far distance I heard the sound of the John Deere clanking along with the mechanical rock picker. Twisting my body, I saw both Juan and José several hundred yards below. I began to scream. Like a coyote in a steel trap, I wailed. Jake joined me, tossing his head and howling.

I looked back down. José was still driving the tractor and Juan was walking behind, working. The tractor noise throbbed in my ears. They were so close, yet too far away.

Fear closed in, cold and rigid. Warm blood trickled out of my nose and a thick, bloody saliva filled my mouth, choking me. When I gurgled and tried to raise my head, Jake gently cleaned the mucus with his tongue so I could breath. He whined and put his head on my neck.

"Three days till my birthday," I told Jake and dealt for a moment with the startling possibility that I might not live to be forty-five.

Shock began with dripping sweat and cold chills. Then harsh reality. I tried moving my feet but couldn't feel them. *If I make it until dark, I'll probably lose my legs.* I screamed one last time.

With my head resting on the rocks and the sun burning, I stared at Jake. I held my hand out and he licked my fingers. "Shorty? Shorty, is that you fella?"

It was 1957, I was ten, a fifth grader at Braden School. I kept walking every few minutes to the pencil sharpener to see if Mama's car was gone, to glance at Shorty, who always waited at the edge of the field. When the station wagon disappeared in a cloud of red dust, I burst out the doors and tore across the school yard, jerking my dog into my arms.

Teacher followed. Miss Hedberg took me by the hand and petted my little friend. "Any dog who comes to school faithfully every day should be learning something," she said, then she officially enrolled Shorty as the first "canine student" in Braden School. My buddy was with me.

Shooting pains in my legs brought me back from the

past. I tried to raise my head, but dehydration and dizziness held me against the ground. I squinted at the sun through swollen eyelids. Had two hours past? Three? Williams might miss me by dark, an eternity away. Jake nuzzled me with his nose and licked me. His damp tongue felt icy cold on my sunburned skin. I put my arms around him and pulled him down to my neck.

I began the Lord's Prayer, but felt hypocritical and stopped. Over the years I'd been the only person I could count on. Me, Myself, and I.

"It isn't my style to grovel in last minute regrets," I said, through chattering teeth. "If You are who You say You are . . . help me!" My throat was parched and my words hoarse. I paused and felt a trickle of blood from my cracked lips. I touched it with my tongue and took it into my mouth for its moisture.

Whispered words came clearly into my ear, "Hang on, Sissy." My dad's voice. Daddy, who'd died, crushed beneath his tractor in the field.

The sound of Dad's tractor came vividly into my mind. He was plowing on the old farm and I was walking toward him, barefoot through the soft dirt with a mason jar of cold tea. The ice was jingling as I walked. Dad saw me, stopped his tractor and waved.

"Good to see you, Sissy."

The urge to live bubbled back inside of me. "I have to write it," I slurred to Jake. "I have to live to write the story."

"Awoony Bawla Caw. Soma Sina Woo Choo," I choked, marking my face with dust. Geronimo stood up in my mind.

Deep crevices of agony in his old face, thin lips drawn solemnly into a straight line, and a squint of determination.

Jake licked my hand and nudged me with his muzzle.

"Okay, Shorty, let's go to the river. I'm so thirsty, boy."

A great sense of peace and belonging replaced all the pain. A cloud shadowed the sun and a fresh breeze cooled me.

Jake barked. A few minutes later Juan lifted the machine off of me and José carried me down the hill.

When I opened my eyes the next morning in the hospital, I asked about Jake.

"He's fine." Williams' face was pale. "Jake saved your life, Okie."

"What?" I asked. "How?"

"Just before dark when Juan went into the lower pasture to feed the mares, Jake grabbed him by the leg. At first, Juan was afraid the dog had gone mad and was attacking him, so he tried to get away. But Jake kept coming at him then ran a few steps barking. Finally, Juan realized Jake wanted him to follow. The dog led him straight up the side of the mountain to you. It was a miracle."

"A miracle?" For a few brief moments I considered the possibility. Right before my rescue, I remembered vividly the sense of Love with all things and I had asked Him to help me.

By the time I left the hospital, I convinced myself that God had nothing to do with any of it. Jake deserved all the credit. But I began to sneak peeks at the Bible while I sat endless hours in the recliner healing. Began to wonder if maybe, just maybe my life did hold some meaning.

Jake became the focus of my existence. After a week, I was able to limp out to his pen. Three weeks after the accident, when I let him out, he ran to the four-wheeler and lay beside it. I called him, but he ignored me. When I hobbled toward him, he barked out encouragement.

Before many weeks had passed, I was on the machine, puttering along the trail with Jake bouncing beside me. He'd slop into the stream, chasing trout shadows while I sat with my bruised legs in the icy water.

Late one August evening, two short months after the accident, Jake and I were walking in the east meadow by the stream. A large doe jumped the fence and darted in front of us. Jake lit out with every fiber of his strong body, stretching, reaching, gaining, his heart on fire with the hunger to be in front.

The neighbor down the country road tried to swerve when he saw the flash of brown and white, but Jake caught the full impact of the truck's front wheel.

I held him in my arms on the way to the vet, reassuring him, but I knew the Big Goof was leaving me. The energy was gone from his passionate eyes. His last lick to my hand was feeble.

My husband and Juan buried Jake above the meadow as I watched in stunned silence. Williams tried to comfort me, but the hole in my heart couldn't be filled.

Then one brilliant October afternoon, I felt Jake calling me to the place where he rested—luring me with his patient, relentless eyes. Numbly, I gathered white flat rocks, covering the mound of bare earth then stumbled blindly down toward the meadow.

Near the stream, something caught my attention. Dog tracks were baked into the clay bank like fossils preserved in rock.

"Jake," I choked, and thought immediately of that poem, "Footprints in the Sand."

I heard a rustling sound and turned. Shorty and Jake were walking toward me and behind them were all of the animals I'd loved in my lifetime. They gathered around me and a strong sense of rapture engulfed me. I knew that the answer to all things was love.

God hadn't abandoned me during the tough times. He'd sent special guardians. Jake and Shorty were kindred spirits. In a strange way I'd known it since the first day I looked into Jake's eyes.

The Big Goof had come to connect me to the past and heal the memories. To link me back to love and trust. Jake was an angel in disguise.

Epilogue

AFTER THE ACCIDENT, IN SEPTEMBER 1993, WILLIAMS AND I traveled to New Mexico to attend the All American Quarter Horse Futurity, an event that has been dubbed the Kentucky Derby of quarter horse racing. Since the trip was a last minute decision, we had not made motel reservations, only to find upon arrival that every room within fifty miles was reserved. Deciding to drive to a neighboring town, we came upon a sign on a back road that said Inn of the Mountain Gods.

"Doesn't that sound beautiful?" I asked, turning on impulse toward the inn.

"Okie," Williams said looking up from the All American Horse Sale catalog, "anything this close to the race track will be full."

The inn was a fabulous resort, hidden between towering pines, sitting above a shimmering lake. The establishment was proudly run by the Mescalero Apaches. I smiled to myself walking down the stone steps toward the office. "If Geronimo were here, he'd let me stay," I thought. The lady behind the desk looked at me with steady, dark eyes.

"Ma'am, the rooms for this weekend have been booked for six months." I stared back at her. "Geronimo and I were friends," I told her in a whisper.

A slow smile spread across her face and she whispered back, "You'll never believe this, but we had a cancellation two minutes before you walked in the door. It's a room overlooking the lake."

That weekend, a Navajo artist named Redwing was displaying several of his oils in the lobby of the inn. I greatly admired his work and told him I'd be interested in one of his future paintings. We visited briefly and exchanged business cards.

Redwing called in August, the following year, as I was finishing the rough draft of this book. He would be bringing several pieces of art back to the inn that September, were we coming? When I assured him we were, he hesitated. "For some reason, I can't explain, as I worked on a particular painting, your name kept coming to me. It was the strongest feeling."

I knew he was successful enough, he wasn't simply trying to make a sale, but the comment did strike me as rather odd. Before I had a chance to inquire further, he continued.

"Anyway, I'd be happy to send you pictures of all the work I'm bringing, if you want."

When the photographs of his paintings arrived the following week, I started through them. I knew instantly the one he had connected to me. As I stared at the renegade Indian running from the White Soldiers, I rubbed the chill bumps from my arms.

In late September, at the Inn of the Mountain Gods, I purchased the painting, entitled, "Fire within Stronghold." It is a splendid likeness of my old friend, Geronimo.

About the Author

Lou Dean Jacobs Williams divides her time between her husband's quarter horse ranch in northeastern Utah and her writing retreat on Blue Mountain in Colorado. She and her husband, Robert Williams, enjoy raising and training quarter horses for racing.

A free-lance writer for twenty years, Lou Dean's work has appeared on the pages of more than fifty magazines. She teaches creative writing classes at Colorado Northeastern Community College, in Rangely, Colorado, and is nearing completion of her bachelor of arts degree at Utah State University.